NAZI LESBIAN VAMPIRES

Stephen Hernandez

Dedicated to Natasha who came in the winter and
brought me summer

CONTENTS

CHAPTER ONE

A STAB IN THE DARK

The first point of wisdom is to discern that which is false, and the second, to know that which is true.

—Lactantius

As soon as SS-Gruppenführer Reinhard Heydrich entered the opulent office he could feel the coolness crawling across his skin. It was not surprising considering the two other occupants: Adolf Hitler and Heinrich Himmler. He saluted his Führer and looked into the round spectacles of Himmler, where their mutual hatred was reflected. Hitler always liked to keep his main staff at odds: it meant competition, and competition always brought out the best, or worst, in people. He wondered how much drugs they had consumed between them prior to the meeting. He included himself in the equation which made it all the more difficult to tell. It was going to be one of those meetings: a children's playground roundabout, where you became too dizzy to know who was pushing and who was riding. Everything gravitated toward the center, and at the center was the Führer.

They sat in front of Hitler's huge but spartan desk and waited for their leader to speak. He smiled at them as if they were all old friends. Heydrich tried, unsuccessfully, not to look into those hypnotic, clear blue eyes.

"Reinhard, I have heard you have an interest in the occult," Hitler said. It was a statement, not a question.

Heydrich glanced at Himmler. There was no hint of a reaction on that inscrutable, bureaucratic face. Was this a trap, a set-up by Himmler, or was Hitler testing him?

He decided to opt for the truth, whatever the consequences. He coughed, as if reluctant to make his confession. He had, indeed, a lifelong interest in the occult. Up to now, that interest had been merely of an academic nature, and one he had kept strictly to himself, until he had mistakenly let slip his secret interest to Himmler. He had been drunk at the time and now cursed himself unceasingly for his indiscretion. He disliked Himmler intensely. Heydrich, who considered himself something of an aristocrat, considered the Reichsführer nothing more than a jumped-up chicken farmer. The only thing they agreed on was the need to purify the Germanic race of the loathsome Jews, and even there, Himmler revealed his farmer's instincts on breeding. But people were not chickens, and you could not confine them to ticks in a book.

"Yes, it's true, Mein Führer. I have had a long interest in the occult, but only the myths that are attached to our own glorious Germanic past." He knew mentioning Germany's former glory, however vague, would go down well with the Führer—a hastily devised safety measure. "I consider myself a mere dilettante compared to some." He nodded at Himmler, putting the ball firmly back in the Reichsführer's court.

"Do you think you could harness that power for the Third Reich?" Hitler looked him straight in the eye. Those fanatical eyes held their own occult power.

"I think it might be more complex than that," Heydrich said.

He was sure he could see the beginning of a smirk on Himmler's lips out of the corner of his eye. Nothing was complex to Hitler if he ordered it. He ignored Heydrich's response, which was reassuringly normal for him. Hitler was only ever interested in what *he* said.

"You, no doubt, have heard of the legends of vampires that inhabited the Urals?"

"Yes, I am aware of the legends, Mein Führer, but they are legends. They may have some basis in truth, but I cannot see how they will aid the Third Reich."

There was definitely a slight smirk on Himmler's lips now.

Hitler gave them both a stern look.

"But what if the legends are true? We could have an army of the undead. It would strike fear into every enemy. I don't want legends, Heydrich. I want the real thing," Hitler slammed his fist on the table.

Heydrich knew his fate lay between the fist on the table and the tiny smirk on Himmler's lips. He did not bother to protest the complexities that dealing with the occult would bring. Early in the conversation, Heydrich had realized he was between a rock and a hard place. The mission of finding vampires would go badly for him. He was sure of it, because he was certain that vampires did not exist. They were myths turned into legend and then resurrected by the mad Irish writer Bram Stoker with his novel: *Dracula*. Himmler had set him a trap. If he failed, he would take the blame, but if he were to actually succeed, Himmler would take the final credit. The master had become jealous of the pupil because of the affection and honors the Führer showered on his underling. There was only room for one right-hand man at the Führer's side. Heydrich could quite easily see that it was time for the Führer's medication. The veins on his forehead were throbbing wildly, and he would soon be calling for his faithful personal doctor, Theodor Morell, who was always lurking near the Führer like a second shadow. Heydrich also very much wanted to leave the vicinity of the odious Himmler.

He had no way of denying his knowledge of the occult now, and seeing the enthusiasm bursting through the fanatical, glaring blue eyes of the Führer, he knew he could not back out. He knew this could very possibly just be one of Hitler's passing fads, and if so he stood to lose everything. So, there it was: he was to search for creatures that did not exist whilst, Himmler, no doubt, made the most of his absence to ingratiate himself further with the Führer. But the Reichsführer had not reckoned on his subordinate's innate cunning—Heydrich had already made contingency plans ...

He directed Klein, his chauffeur, to take him directly to the Gestapo Headquarters. The security police headquarters had an extensive document library, but it contained mainly intelligence gathered to deal with the Jewish problem. Heydrich had built a private annex, where he stored some of his own intelligence: ancient tomes of the occult that had never seen the light of day. They told of black arts so heinous that they would turn even a hardened soldier's stomach. But Heydrich was no ordinary man. It was not for nothing that he had gained the nickname *the Hangman*, and he was considered the cruelest and most brutal of the Nazis a reputation not easily gained. Heydrich picked out two of his rarest, most arcane grimoires. The legendary manuscripts had cost the owners their lives. Tracking them down had gone particularly hard for many men, as the Gestapo's torture chambers could testify. When Heydrich wanted a particular book, he got it—no matter how much blood was spilled and pain inflicted in the process.

The two grimoires he selected were: *the Voynich Manuscript* and *the Munich Manual of Demonic Magic*. There were some small illustrations in the *Voynich Manuscript* that had always particularly fascinated him. They would often send shivers down his usual steely spine, as if there were some direct connection to him. The picture was repeated in several different versions throughout the manuscript. It basically consisted of six naked women and a naked man sharing a circular, wooden bathtub that appeared to be filled with blood rather than water. They had secret, flirtatious smiles, sometimes aimed at each other and sometimes, at the man, who could have been their shared master or lover. The illustrations were small and intricate. They could only be truly appreciated with a powerful magnifying glass. It was by this method that Heydrich could observe what made the figures so frightening—it was their eye teeth. They were pointed and sharp, and they looked too large for their mouths, resembling fangs rather than normal dentures. This fact had always interested Heydrich. Perhaps it was the oldest illustration of so-called vampires that existed. He intended to make it the starting point of his quest.

The grimoire was considered to be one of the most mysterious manuscripts in the history of mankind. It contained a ciphered, unknown, alphabet written on vellum. The fact, that had most interested Heydrich was that the foremost scholar of that strange alphabet lived in Berlin. The only problem was that the professor, or rather, the former professor, was a Jew. He had been stripped of his position because of the *Abnenpass* measures—he had failed to provide sufficient proof of Aryan ancestry. The fact that this applied to nearly half of the high-ranking Nazis was blithely overlooked. Once you were in the Nazi party, you were *in*. Dealing closely with one of those sub-human *Untermensch* was against all of Heydrich's principles, but it had to be done if he wanted the knowledge he sought.

Heydrich had purposely kept the old man alive for just such an eventuality. He had been certain that at some time, if he wanted to follow his own occult theories, he would need the Jew's help. Now he had been proven correct. Even so, he had still sent the man's family to a concentration camp. He did not want a Jew believing he had gone soft. It was also a useful bargaining tool. He told the professor they would remain unharmed while he worked for him, but he had already had them all gassed immediately upon their arrival at Belzec. It gave him no small satisfaction that the old man was unaware that he was working for the chief of the Gestapo for nothing, an empty promise.

He ordered two of his men to bring the professor up from his cell in the basement, which had been converted into a makeshift research room for the Jew.

"Well, what have you got for me?", he demanded.

The frail old man shrank back into the metallic chair in which he had been planted as if he wanted to become part of its frame.

"There is still a long way to go, sir. So difficult ... Please ..."

"Do you want to see your family again, rat?"

The old man looked up tearfully. His swollen eyes fell upon one of Heydrich's many rare books lying open on the Obergruppenführer's desk.

"Is that the Oera Linda?", he asked, timidly, as if he expecting a blow.

Heydrich glared down at him.

"That book does not concern you. I asked you a question. How much have you managed to translate?"

"It ... it ... is not so much a question of translation. If you could tell me what you are looking for, I may have some threads." The old man waved his spaghetti-thin arms helplessly.

Heydrich sat down and glowered at him. He put his boots on the desk, directly in line with the Jew's face, as if he could stamp on it forever. He knew many interrogation methods and he knew he would not get the information he wanted by using force. The man was too weak, like all of his kind, and would give him any sort of answer to stop a painful beating. He needed the old man to open up, and for that, he needed to make him comfortable. He ordered in some sandwiches and coffee, and he watched in disgust as the old man shoveled the food into his mouth, hardly bothering to chew, like the filthy animal he was. It really was a nauseating sight. When the old man had finished Heydrich offered him a cigarette from his silver cigarette case. The old man took it with trembling hands and Heydrich lit it for him with an equally elegant silver lighter. Heydrich had been surrounding himself with a lot of silver lately—a precaution.

"Now I will tell you what I am looking for, and you will help me find it. You will stay here in this office. You will sleep, eat, and shit here, until you have found it. You will have access to writings you can only ever have dreamed about."

Heydrich told him of his quest to find vampires, how he believed the strange painting of the figures in the bathtubs in the *Voynich Manuscript* to be his only real link. He did not trust fictional works, such as those of the drunkard Bram Stoker, although, some element of truth might lie in them. After all, there had been stories of so-called *night walkers* that sucked blood, throughout Great Britain, as early as medieval times. It was the Jew's job to find out if they truly existed and where Heydrich might find them. He wanted an exact location—time was of the essence.

He then led the dazed old man into his private annex and showed him his collection. The professor's tired old eyes lit up behind his spectacles as he made out the titles. He stroked their covers reverentially. He gasped ...

"The Red Dragon—The Grand Grimoire! But there is only one copy, and it is kept by the pope himself in the Vatican."

Heydrich gave the professor one of his enigmatic smiles that he reserved for those who doubted his power.

"Yes, so there *was.* Now, get to work." With that, he marched out of his office.

Professor Leibowitz gazed around in wonder. A strange contentment fell over him. It was not just because of the books and manuscripts—after all, that was the world he was accustomed to. It was the luxury of his surroundings and having a full stomach. It brought back a host of memories. He fought back the tears that were filling his eyes. He had to get on with his work, not only to get his family back, but also to destroy the Nazis. Unlike Heydrich, he was not a skeptic. He firmly believed in vampires. If Nazis existed, then why not vampires? There was plenty of room in the world for more monsters.

It was the professor's fervent hope that he could discover the whereabouts of some real vampires, because, from what he knew of the legendary creatures they were as much to be trusted as Heydrich himself. He was quite certain that he had little hope of seeing his family again. Heydrich, would most certainly have him killed once he had given him the information he needed. Nevertheless, he lived with the vain, fervent hope that he might save his family. And the professor knew, somehow, that if Heydrich found real vampires, they would not only eventually kill him, but would bring the whole of the Third Reich tumbling down around him and his beloved Führer.

In the days that followed the old man's strength grew due to decent food and being left undisturbed. He worked tremendously hard. On the third day, when Heydrich interviewed him, he had some important information for him.

Heydrich felt his spine tingle as the old Jew told him of his discoveries. It seemed that the bathtubs were being filled with blood from intricate pipes, and their mysterious occupants, six females and one man, were indeed vampires. The females were sexually ambiguous. They had all been made vampires by their master, the male, who shared in their bloody orgy. The Jew explained that the bathtubs represented the vampires' world which was filled with blood and sex. The key point about the illustrations, and the enigmatic references to them, was that they seemed to be partly based on fact and partly on prophecy. The vampires lived in a timeless realm. Immortal, they came and went as they saw fit. He also pointed out something that Heydrich had missed in the illustrations. The logical part of his mind had subconsciously deemed it of little interest— a small drawing of a black bell that appeared randomly throughout the manuscript.

The professor had used several other books and grimoires to follow up on this particular theme. It was in an ancient, untitled manuscript, so old and fragile that he had to use tweezers to read it lest it crumble to dust, that he had found the answer he had been searching for. He found mention of a Count and his six concubines who dwelt in a ruined castle deep in Transylvania. The master of the vampires might even be related to *Vlad the Impaler*, who was sometimes known by the name of Count Dragwlya. This was a name that had substantial connections with the ancient Order of the Dragon. An order many believed to have its origins in the legends of Saint George who upon killing the great serpent had been cursed to walk the lands in perpetuity, only gaining sustenance from blood itself.

It was at this point that Heydrich stopped the Jew's account by getting to his feet and slamming his fist on the desk, causing the old man to start violently. Thunderbolts of anger flashed from his normally cold ice blue eyes.

"Are you mocking me, Jew? I've read *Dracula* by Bram Stoker as well. Do you take me for a fool?"

He leaned over his desk and peered directly into the old man's eyes. His voice was calm now.

"Do you know there is a small room in this building that contains one thing and one thing only: a down sized guillotine designed by a Herr Johann Reichhart for executing prisoners we have no more time for. More specifically, prisoners I have no more time for. It is far more frightening and intimidating than any firing squad. We have to strap the prisoners to gurneys to keep them still. Sometimes we strap them in face up so they can see the blade and their fate reflected upon it. The guards run a book on how long it will take for the prisoners to shit themselves. It's amazing how much they scream for mercy. We had to have the room sound-proofed so it would not upset the female staff."

Heydrich relaxed back in his comfortable chair, clearly enjoying himself now. "I have often left them lying there for hours with no choice but to look at that razor edge. Trousers full of shit and piss. It really is most gratifying ... Now, explain yourself quickly before you find yourself staring at that blade."

The professor stared Heydrich straight in the eyes. His strength of character, which had at one time been formidable, had been partly restored, along with physical strength.

"I do not know where Bram Stoker gained his information. Maybe ... he got part of it from the same sources ... embroidered the rest. But not all of his novel is fictional. I'm sure of that. Here is my full report." He handed Heydrich a dark grey folder. "It contains a map of the location of the count's castle."

Heydrich noted this new found strength of character. There were not many men who could meet his gaze, and for most of them, it was the last thing they ever saw.

It took him an hour to read through the folder. The professor sat motionless the whole time. Finally, Heydrich finished the report. He was extremely satisfied. In fact, he was practically bursting with excitement. It seemed the old Jew had accomplished the impossible. But he said nothing, merely pressed the intercom and barked some orders. Three burly men wearing thick brown aprons and large rubber gloves, marched into the room and grabbed the old man. They dragged him, struggling and protesting, out of the room and into the corridor.

He shouted, "I did what you asked!" as the door firmly shut.

The men threw him onto the waiting gurney and strapped him face up with practiced movements. They wheeled him down the cold gray corridor. All the old man could do was stare at the glaring ceiling lights as they rapidly passed overhead like the broken white lines in the middle of a road. He was pushed into a room through a swinging door. He could hardly move his head but could just make out a man incongruously wearing a black coat, white shirt and gloves, black bow tie, and top hat—an executioner's formal attire. The professor wondered in his terror if it was Johann Reichhart. He felt like asking, but his jaw refused to open. Plastic curtains were drawn. The next moment, he found himself staring at the brilliantly shiny, triangular blade of the guillotine. The executioner wasted no time. He looked at his pocket watch, raised his arm, and brought it down in a chopping motion. There was a hum as the blade fell—then blackness.

Heydrich contentedly lit a cigarette. The intercom buzzed. He was informed that the execution had been carried out. He acknowledged the "Heil Hitler" and clicked it off. He could not have anyone sharing the credit for the findings in the folder, especially not a Jew. He couldn't wait to see Himmler's face when he presented it to the Führer.

He was right about Himmler's reaction. The Reichsführer smiled in congratulation, but Heydrich could see the annoyance behind Himmler's round spectacles. It nearly turned into a scowl when Hitler told Heydrich of the rewards, medals, and promotion he could expect if he returned with the vampires as comrades-in-arms. Heydrich vowed to do so even if it meant waking the dead.

CHAPTER TWO

A WALK IN THE WOODS

Come to the woods, for here is rest. There is no repose like that of the green deep woods. Sleep in forgetfulness of all ill

John Muir

Hitler gave Heydrich his own small, secret, and elite SS Panzer unit. It was to penetrate the Carpathian Mountain range in Romania and make its way to Transylvania without engaging in conflict, if at all possible. The unit's mission was to escort the vampires, *if* Heydrich should find and befriend them, safely back to Berlin. Heydrich found the unit to be rather sullen. They did not like the fact that their orders were so vague. No one knew what was going on, and this was something they were not accustomed to. The elite SS soldiers liked to be psyched up before they went into battle. Uncertainty played on their minds as rumors circulated about a secret mission. Still, they felt honored to be commanded by such a high-profile officer as Heydrich. Plus, they had all been issued extra rations of methamphetamine in the form of the immensely popular Pervitin pills. The Waffen SS considered their soldiers to be animated engines, and Pervitin was their fuel. The engines were primed and ready to go ...

The general addressed his men and gave them such an inspiring speech that the unit's spirit was restored. Now, they were eager to be on the move, proud that they had been chosen for a secret mission that was of such vital importance to the Fatherland. They swore to follow their leader to the end of the world and through the gates of Hell itself if necessary. Little did they know that was exactly where they were heading.

It was hard getting the tanks across the Carpathians. Most of the roads were not designed for motorized vehicles, let alone tanks. The narrow dirt roads were bordered by sheer drops or walls of rock, and a lot of the time, they had to smash their way through forests or cut a path using chain saws. The infantry wandered through the dark woods. The trees were huge, and blocked out all sunlight, turning everything a dark, aquamarine green as if they were submerged in the depths of the ocean. There was the familiar smell of permanent autumn and Aesculus hippocastanum (the professor's label on the map for horse-chestnut), but most of all, there was the smell of decay, of death without the promise of resurrection.

The Jewish professor had only managed to produce a crude and rudimentary map of the castle's location, but so far it had proven reasonably precise. Even so, they terrorized many villages on their way just by stopping to ask directions. One town they passed through was known as Bran. The townsfolk could not believe that they really were not there to massacre them. There was a grand castle, but not the one Heydrich sought.

Weeks passed until, finally, Heydrich was leading the Panzer regiment toward a remote village deep within the Carpathian mountains along the bandit-ridden border between Transylvania and Wallachia. Only the most dedicated scholars of the occult would have heard of it. The inhabitants could hear the huge iron machines approaching from a long distance away. The very foundations of their houses shook. They had heard rumors about the far-off war from refugees who had managed to escape the carnage only to disappear without a trace into the surrounding deep forest. This was despite the fact that the villagers had warned them that it was probably safer to face men, however dangerous and cruel, than what lay in the forest.

Heydrich left the tanks and most of the men on the outskirts of the village. He did not want to terrify the locals too much. They were not here to kill, only to seek information. The tanks were merely there to suggest that if he did not get the information he wanted then there would be no more village.

He arrived in what he presumed was the center of the village. It had no name on the maps of the world and consisted of only a dozen or so houses. It was deserted. He had the hulking Klein loudly boom the klaxon horn of the large, armor-plated Mercedes. Some doors tentatively opened. Faces peered from behind window shutters or cracks in doorways. Heydrich had brought an interpreter with him and he ordered him to shout that they came in peace. It would have looked dubious to any objective observer given the amount of weaponry his surrounding bodyguards were armed with, but the villagers were not really used to such modern weapons. They mistook them for the kind of old rifles that some of the woodsmen would hunt with. Maybe they were just hunters, they thought, hunters who had lost their way, although, their clothing was ill-fitting and strange for huntsmen, who usually wished to remain unseen.

A very old man who, Heydrich presumed, was the village leader finally came out of what appeared to be the only tavern in the village. It also served as the only, seldom-used, inn. He hobbled toward the tall man in the strange, black costume and his speaker. He guessed that the tall man with the cold, ice-blue eyes of a killer was the one in authority.

He was dressed in a gruesome outfit bedecked with death's heads, which the old man presumed was somehow meant to be intimidating. The old man, though, was not the least fearful of the strange man, or what he represented. He had seen more frightening things in his time, much, much more frightening, and he had survived them—against all odds. But curiosity had got the better of him. He wondered what the strange man was doing in his village.

"Can I help you, sir?" he asked politely.

"We are looking for a castle. We hear it lies in these forests," Heydrich said through the interpreter.

"A castle?" the old man said innocently, as though he had never heard of such a thing.

"Yes, you know, a big stone building shaped like a fortress ... Do you want me to draw you a picture?"

"There is one such place, but it is mere ruins. No one ever goes there. What's the point of visiting old stones?"

"We would like to see it all the same ... I'm something of a sightseer and I don't mind ruins—or creating them." Heydrich glanced nonchalantly around the small group of wooden houses.

The old man bowed in an odd, submissive manner, not unlike a serf to his master. He beckoned them obsequiously into the rustic tavern.

"I will tell you something about this place you

seek. Perhaps I can dissuade you from going there ... I think it would be best for everyone, especially your estimable self."

He had them all served ale in ancient pewter tankards. Heydrich found it quite palatable, but much darker and bitter than the beer he was used to. A shriveled shrew of an old woman served them. When she wasn't waiting upon them, she spent the rest of the time crossing herself and kissing a crucifix.

Heydrich noticed the place was hung everywhere with garlic,. He'd had an inkling he had found the right place according to his studies and the professor's help, and now he was sure of it.

"Do you eat a lot of garlic here?" he enquired. "I thought only the French did that."

"A local superstition, I'm afraid," the old man said, "to ward off strigoi, although I'm afraid it would be of little use. *If* ... they existed, of course. Just legends, but you know how these things persist—we are far from the modern world here. Anyway, the garlic flowers would be of much better use against *them* ... but, who listens to an old man."

"We call them vampires ... Just tell me about the castle, or your little village will also pass into legend," ... Heydrich growled with impatience.

He had grown bored. He didn't want superstitions now. He wanted facts, and he knew instinctively that the old man knew the ones he wanted.

So, the old man told him the facts as far as he knew them. As the story unfolded many of the soldiers found themselves going off their ale. The tales the old man told, although paranormal in the extreme, had an unmistakable ring of authenticity. When he had finished, he asked Heydrich a simple question.

"Do you still want to go to the ruins of that castle? If you do ... I would advise you go by daylight but return by sundown. You may lay this village and all in it to waste if you wish ... if you feel I have lied to you. I would rather that than you unleash what is contained there."

They stayed the night at the inn. It would be impractical to take the tanks through such a thick forest, and then there was, according to the old man, some sort of mountain to contend with. On top of that, Heydrich did not want to announce his approach. The old man had managed to secure them a very frightened guide. He was to lead Heydrich, and some of the Waffen SS to where the ruins of the castle lay. He insisted that as soon as he had pointed out its location he would return to the village, even on pain of death.

Heydrich felt triumphant. It had taken him a lot of painstaking research to find this place, or rather, it had taken the Jewish professor ... but it had been worth it. At last he had the result he had so desperately sought. He was on the verge of something extraordinary, something only he, the magnificent Heydrich, could have accomplished. He could practically smell the wet *mösen* of the adoring, *schöne frauen* who would be queuing up for his attention when he arrived back in Berlin. His mouth watered in anticipation.

Once they had gotten into the depths of the forest it was difficult to tell if they were in daylight or not. The Kübelwagens were crawling at walking pace. There was just enough space to navigate between the ivied boles of the huge trees. Slinking shadows weaved in and out the dark olive undergrowth. The soldiers were pretty sure they were wolves—they moved much too quickly and smoothly for humans. All of them had their machine guns at the ready. Finally, they emerged from the woods ...

CHAPTER THREE

WAKING THE DEAD

The blood is life!

Bram Stoker

The sky was shrouded in clouds of heavy mist. Heydrich left most of the men behind with the vehicles at the foot of the "mountain," which was little more than a glorified vertical hill. True to his word, the guide immediately left them. Heydrich was tempted to chain the man up, but he was in a benevolent mood. He even allowed the interpreter to go with him. If they really had found the vampires he sought, something told him that the interpreter would be superfluous. He put Klein in charge until he returned. He took a small group of his best men with him up to the castle, on foot. It was a steep and vertiginous climb, as there did not appear to be any road or even a path to the castle. If there was, or had been, it had long since disappeared in the wild undergrowth. The place did not even meet his lowest expectations. It was more ruinous than any ruin he had ever seen and Heydrich had seen and created a good many. It exhaled decay. There was not even a hint of past glories. Just death.

He was severely disappointed. It had obviously been uninhabited for countless years. The Jew bastard must have known, and he was probably laughing in his unmarked grave at that very moment. How Heydrich wished he had the rat with him now. He would make sure his death agony lasted for weeks—he had been too soft giving the shit such a quick end. He kicked a stone in frustration, sending it flying over the precipice. He looked around in his fury to kick another one and suddenly noticed the bare, square patch of earth he was standing on. It was perfectly symmetrical. There was no growth of weeds or moss, unlike all the other parts of the ruin. Then he understood ...

His second-in-command approached hesitantly.

"Sir, we have enough daylight left to get back to the village."

"Don't be ridiculous! Are you afraid of some illiterate peasant's superstitions? We came here for a purpose. I don't care if it's night or day. We have rations for a week. We will stay here that long if necessary. We will camp here the night. Issue the men double rations of Pervitin."

Just as the SS-Obersturmbannführer marched away to bark orders at the men, Heydrich asked him. "Haven't you noticed there is something strange about the architecture in this spot?"

The SS-Obersturmbannführer turned around. "No sir. Why?"

"Most of the center walls are more or less intact. It's the surrounding walls that have crumbled away ... There's something deeper than just a foundation under this place. I think there are chambers underneath the center. Maybe ... there were once dungeons. Let the men have their rations ... Then start digging."

They dug late into the night and the early hours of the morning. And then they found it—a trapdoor. Surprisingly heavy, it took six of his strongest men to get it open. It had been bolted, from the inside ...

Once opened, it revealed a winding staircase leading deep underground. The surrounding walls had been very solidly constructed, almost too solidly—as if it were a vault. There were sulfur and lime torches in iron sconces lining the staircase, which, surprisingly, considering their obvious antiquity, lit very well. The place smelled of the rotting damp of the earth itself. Like a grave, Heydrich couldn't help thinking. When they reached the bottom of the seemingly never-ending stairwell, they were presented with another obstacle: an extremely heavy door reinforced with iron straps and bolts. It also appeared locked from the inside. Heydrich ordered it blown open.

Once the smoke had cleared they removed the door. It took the strength of all the men, including Heydrich, to shift it to one side. Inside was some kind of ancient crypt or tomb. But it was no ordinary crypt. It contained the most exquisite furniture and artwork. It could have been the living room of a prince— except for the tombs. There were seven, arranged in a circle. The largest, most elegant was in the middle, and the others surrounded it. Heydrich walked warily around the tombs. He noticed that the central tomb had Zoroastrian inscriptions on it, but his knowledge of that ancient, dark language was limited. He could not translate their meaning. However, all of the tombs had the same Latin inscription: *"Non videre sed esse"*—"To exist but not be seen."

Even his battle-hardened men were nervous in this eerie crypt. One of them even exclaimed, "This is an unholy place!"

"We are not on God's work here, but the Führer's. He is your God as far as you are concerned. This place is not unholy ... What we are about to do maybe ... Those who have no stomach for it may leave now—I will deal with them later." No one moved.

He ordered the casket of holy water they had brought with them to be sprinkled around the tombs. Every man had been issued a large crucifix, which they all now placed around their necks. Heydrich took out his own special protection against whatever lay inside the tomb. It was said by mystics to be the most powerful crucifix in the world, a silver cross that, according to legend, had been worn by Vlad the Impaler himself before he had turned away from the Church. Heydrich collected such mystic items, with or without their rightful owners' consent. It was his most prized possession.

With great difficulty, they managed to pry open the lid of the central tomb with a crowbar. It was lined with scarlet velvet that seemed not to have an aged a day. More extraordinary still, it contained the healthy but pale body of an extremely handsome elderly man. He was dressed in very elegant, outmoded clothes and appeared to be peacefully sleeping.

Suddenly, his eyes sprang open, revealing clear, deep blue eyes. He sat upright, and stifled a yawn. He looked around at the soldiers.

"Ah, breakfast," he said in perfect, if somewhat archaic, German, and he rose from the tomb without having to move his limbs. The horrified soldiers leaped back, their rifles at the ready. Only the Gruppenführer kept his cool.

"Wait!" Heydrich said. "If you are who I believe you to be—I have come to you as a friend ... with a proposition that will be of great benefit to both of us. I was sent by our leader, who hopes to furnish you with as many victims as you desire." Heydrich played his trump card: "Without retribution ... "

"I take it by your bizarre dress that you are wearing some kind of uniform. I must say I like the death's heads ... if a trifle in bad taste. What century is this? And you may address me as Count."

"The twentieth ... Count."

"Is there a war again?" the Count asked, stifling another yawn. He had appeared right beside Heydrich before the Gruppenführer had time to blink. "There usually is ... somewhere or other."

"Yes, a world war, which we are winning ... If you aid us, our Führer will make sure you are suitably compensated ... in whatever fashion you desire."

The Count appeared to be considering. "Tell me more about this Führer of yours."

Heydrich told him, and he found himself telling him much more than he wanted to. The Count seemed to be making the words flow out of him as if he had turned on a tap that, however much he tried, Heydrich could not turn back off. He found himself confessing to Hitler's manic mood swings, his utter ruthlessness, his lack of empathy, and the burning hatred that always lurked beneath the thinly disguised surface. His men were stunned. Something was wrong—they had never heard a superior officer, especially one as loyal as Heydrich, talk like this about their great Führer.

"Hmmm ... " the Count said, stroking his finely kept mustache and goatee. "The man sounds promising."

He waved his hand at the other tombs. "And what of my 'girls'—my concubines?"

Even as he spoke, there were grating noises from the other sarcophagi. To the further horror of the soldiers, the heavy stone lids rose effortlessly by themselves.

Heydrich ordered his men to remain calm in his most authoritative voice. He didn't like the way some fingers were twitching on triggers. His Stabs Feldwebel reinforced the message by barking at the now plainly terrified soldiers. They had seen most of the atrocities war could throw at them, but they were not prepared for anything like this.

They had no more need of orders, though—they visibly relaxed. Instead of strange men with uncanny powers, there arose from the stone coffins a half-dozen of the most beautiful women the soldiers had ever seen. Even Heydrich's normally square-jawed demeanor dropped. He considered the charms of women superfluous except when it came to his personal gratification or the greater glory of the Fatherland. Their main duty, as far as he was concerned, was to satiate his lust and produce more pure Aryan soldiers for the future. More wars were inevitable if the Third Reich was to rule the whole world, and they would need many more soldiers.

"These are my 'girls'," the Count said casually. "I will spare the introductions. I am sure even your disciplined men must have need of female company once in a while ... I assure you they are all quite willing and very hungry for a man's body."

The 'girls' smiled sweetly at the soldiers. Shudders of pleasure involuntarily shot through the men's bodies.

Heydrich was in a quandary. Should he let his men have their pleasure or order them to stand to attention as was befitting in the presence of ladies? But he noticed many of them were already standing at attention in an entirely different manner. These beauties, whatever they were, seemed to be able to seduce at will.

"I will let them have their way with your women *if* you agree to the contract with my Führer ... Otherwise ... we will leave now and leave you to your *peace*." Heydrich had decided on calling the Count's   bluff.

"You have my word on that. And believe me, I keep my word—as long as the other party does as well." The Count sounded terribly reassuring.

He led Heydrich to a pair of ornate, gilded chairs in a corner of the room. A part, even if very minute, of Heydrich's stubborn nature wanted to join in this unearthly delight, but he could not sink to the level of his subordinates ... It would not do. His dalliances were kept strictly behind closed doors.

"I trust your army has many soldiers?" the Count asked nonchalantly as he scrutinized his well-manicured nails.

"Enough to conquer the world twice over," was Heydrich's overzealous reply.

The Count nodded slightly.

"So, they won't miss a few, will they?

"I don't know what you mean," answered a perplexed Heydrich. They had seemed to have been getting along pretty well as far as he was concerned, and he was already imagining the delight on Hitler's face—the decorations and promotion he would receive ... and Himmler scowling in the background. But the atmosphere seemed to have grown quite cold and silent. It was as if time had stopped for a moment and he were a mute witness to a well-rehearsed play. He was paralyzed in the chair, an unmoving statue— his limbs had turned to stone. He knew it was the Count's doing, and deep inside he knew what the Count's words meant. He was glad he was powerless. It was too terrible to contemplate, and not to act. Heydrich would write later in his personal diary, "If I ever had any lingering fear of hell, it is gone, for this day I have seen it with my own eyes." What he was about to see would haunt him for the rest of his life.

"You see, my 'girls' will be most hungry after such a long sleep, although their preferences in other matters we will not discuss at this moment." The Count turned his head slowly toward Heydrich. "I will let you live, Herr Heydrich, because I am bored with my sleep. I would like to see how the world has progressed in my absence, and see this Third Reich, as you call it. What you witness here will show you the power we possess, our true nature, which you dare to unleash. You're really quite a silly man."

A beautiful half-caste young woman had already released the Feldwebel's penis from the restrictive confines of his uniform trousers. He looked down in stupefaction as one of the most beautiful women he had ever seen in his life, or indeed, in his dreams, prepared to pleasure him—and not even at bayonet point! Her cupid shaped mouth with such full and luscious lips opened to receive him. Just as he was preparing himself for the inevitable, pleasurable sensation of untapped release (his orgasm had already begun), he found, instead, his mouth contorting in a rictus of utter dismay. The Feldwebel let forth shrieks of such intensity they seemed to rebound off the solid walls—echoes ladened with horror. She had bitten his penis completely off, right down to his testicles. She spat it out in disgust, as if it were rotten meat. The stunned, shocked troops looked on as she opened her mouth wide and greedily drank the fountain of dark blood now gushing from the hole where his penis had been while, at the same time from one side of her mouth, spat out his jism.

If they had cared to ask, she, Selene, could have told them she was well-practiscd in that particular form of dispatching male victims. As a young girl, when she was still mortal and, living in a small seaside village in the Caribbean, she had learned to scavenge and eat live crabs with their shells still on, sucking and swallowing the meat and juices, pushing the pieces of shell with her dextcrous tongue to form a ball in the side of her cheek, and then spitting it out. She still remembered those days in the sun when she was hungry because she had always been hungry then. That was before she had met the Count and Angelique ...

The soldiers tried to react quickly: pulling up their trousers and reaching for their machine guns, rifles, daggers or anything else they had around them they could use as a weapon. They now realized that it was not sex the females wanted, well, not the kind they were used to anyway, and that they killed once their lust was fulfilled—much like the soldiers themselves. But the manner was grotesque—they had never witnessed sanguivores feeding before. The holy water and crucifixes seemed useless here—they were disdainfully ignored by the vampires. The soldiers vigorous training and sense of survival took over, but to the vampires it was as if the men were moving in strobed slow motion, and within seconds they had pounced on the erstwhile, lustful soldiers—now just trying to defend their lives. They did not just bury their perfect teeth in their necks, as legends would have it, but bit wherever blood would flow, and within seconds, they sucked all the men dry of that necessary fluid, leaving pale shriveled corpses. It might have come as some late consolation to the soldiers that the "girls" were so hungry that they did not even bother to transmogrify into their true vampire selves—that would have been truly monstrous.

Heydrich found he could still neither speak nor move a muscle. The Count had not released him from the paralyzing spell. All he could do was look on in stupefied consternation. The vampires brought the only surviving soldier to the Count. He was quivering with fear despite all his medals for bravery in combat. The Count, in one sweeping, almost elegant movement, ripped out the man's throat and drained him in seconds. He let the pale corpse flop to the floor like an empty sack. It had all happened in the blink of an eye, but it had seemed like an eternity for the SS-Gruppenführer. He had watched helplessly as his men were slaughtered, bled like pigs in an abattoir.

"Your mind is sailing the seas of an emotional storm, Herr Heydrich," the Count said. "Ignore it."

He turned his head slowly towards Heydrich, his lips still crimson from the blood feast.

"Now, do you understand? By the way, if you think that little trinket in your hand will save you from me you are sadly mistaken. It might work on lesser vampires, but I was *created* before it was forged, even before the rise of Christendom itself."

"Created?" Heydrich, rasped, as the power of speech returned to his raw throat.

"Oh, yes, we are *made* by other vampires, but only older vampires, *Nosferatu*, have that power." He smiled benevolently at Heydrich, as if he a were kindly old tutor instructing a schoolboy still in shorts. After the scene Heydrich had witnessed, it made it all the more sinister.

"We aren't born like this. Although ... sometimes I think one of us must have been ... a freak of nature ... perhaps. A bizarre offshoot of evolution, do you think?" he asked with genuine curiosity. "I was *made* so long ago I've even forgotten my own name. I was a count ... or the equivalent ... at one time. That ... seems to be all that remains of my mortal self. I do not even remember my maker ... if I met him or her now ... I'm not sure if I would thank them. Mortal life is so much simpler. My powers have increased with age ... My memory, sadly, has not." He sighed wistfully. "Maybe ... it's just as well."

"We will travel with you to your homeland. Your remaining soldiers will remove our wooden traveling coffins from that alcove." He indicated a shadowy corner of the room. "We will presently occupy them. I urge you not to be tempted to open them during the journey. We like to sleep, especially during the day, and do not like to be disturbed. If you do ... well ... you have seen the consequences."

Heydrich forced his still numb lips to speak," Sunlight is fatal to you, is it not?"

The Count waved the question away, "To some ... yes ... but there are certain of us who can resist it, just like your holy water and crucifixes. You are welcome to try the experiment ... You know very little about us Herr Heydrich ... despite all your *research*. We will prepare ourselves for the journey ... The movable items are to travel with us."

Heydrich found himself fully released from whatever hold the Count had on him. He slowly mounted the long, winding staircase in movements that more resembled an automaton than a man.

A grim, pale-faced, and solemn Gruppenführer ordered enough men to go below to retrieve the wooden coffins, which on no account were to be opened, and all the furniture and ornaments that were not fixed. What they saw there was never to be repeated to anyone. There would be no time to bury their fallen comrades, but they could remove any letters or personal effects meant for loved ones back in the Fatherland.

The trip back down the mountain was arduous because of the number of items they had to carry to their vehicles. It was not much better through the forest, driving the now overloaded Kübelwagens once again through that wolf-inhabited shadow-land. They arrived back at the village exhausted. The inhabitants gawped at them as they loaded the objects from the Kübelwagens onto the trucks. When they saw the coffins they started kissing their rudimentary crucifixes, counting rosaries, and reciting long-forgotten prayers. They retreated into their houses and, closed and bolted every door and, every window.

The old man who had first greeted them was the only person left outside. He approached Heydrich with some trepidation, but it was also laced with some anger, an anger that only a fearless old man could muster in the face of the tall SS-Gruppenführer who radiated death. Heydrich was not nicknamed, the "Hangman", for nothing.

"Do you realize what you have done?" the old man said.

"I have won the war for the Fatherland!" Heydrich, replied as he got into his Mercedes. He was so excited he could not even be bothered to shoot the old man for his insolence. He had already dismissed him from his mind.

"No, you have unleashed Hell ... " the old man said to himself. He walked slowly back to his inn, shaking his head all the while, as if he were a mourner in a funeral cortege. If Heydrich had bothered to ask after the ancient's name, which he hadn't, he might have been interested to learn that he was distantly related to a certain Van Helsing.

The trucks pulled away to meet up with their tank escort.

At night, the soldiers watched nervously over the coffins. They did not know what they contained, but they were sure that whatever it was must be dangerous. Their usually stolid Leutnant had told them to report to him immediately if there was any sign of movement—a strange order. All the way back to Germany there was no sound from the coffins, but more unusually, there was no sign of wildlife—not even a rabbit to supplement their rations. It ... seemed as if even the birds had vanished from the skies.

Heydrich had ordered a luxurious château be prepared for the Count and his concubines. Once everything had been arranged as properly as possible, the Count mysteriously rose from his coffin exactly as he had from his tomb. This time, though, it was only Heydrich who was present to witness it. Heydrich informed him that the dungeons contained prisoners of war and some local Jews who had been rounded up—in case they were hungry. The Count appeared to be satisfied with the arrangements. The SS-Gruppenführer left before the vampires began their feasting. He never wished to see such a thing again.

He drove immediately to Berlin to make his report.

This time he was in an exuberant mood when he faced Himmler and Hitler. Hitler had just finished reading the dossier. His face, Heydrich was pleased to see, was plastered with a beaming smile, while, as he had anticipated, Himmler looked far from happy. He was hiding it well, though. It must be hard on the old boy, Heydrich thought gleefully, not being the flavor of the day—he wasn't used to it.

The Führer got up from behind his desk and embraced Heydrich.

"Congratulations, Reinhard. I knew if anyone could do it, it would be you. There is a medal in this for you, and I'm promoting you to SS-Obergruppenführer. Sit down, my boy, sit down."

Himmler's round spectacles looked like they were about to steam up. Heydrich sat down feeling far more comfortable than usual.

"So meiner Komaraden, what suggestions have you got for using our new guests" *gifts*?" Hitler said to them both.

"A graveyard," Himmler said dryly.

Hitler chuckled, but only briefly. "Now, now Heinrich we will have many uses for them ... I suggest ... " Both of them knew that when Hitler "suggested" something, it was tantamount to an order. "We will use them to induce fear," Hitler thumped his fist on the desk to emphasisze every word. "It's the best way to control the weak."

Then came the bombshell Heydrich had been waiting for: Hitler said, "I'm making you, Reinhard, Stellvertretender Reichsprotektor of Bohemia and Moravia ... You will leave for the new Czechoslovakia and your new command immediately. You can install our new allies in the castle at Panenske Brezany ... if you like ... ." Heydrich was aware that Hitler's "if you likes" were exactly the same as his suggestions. "It will help if the superstitious idiots think it is haunted. The more fear ... the better ... Keep the curious away. Begin a reign of terror ... We will have the filthy Jews running to the sewers where they belong ... You will flush the untermenschen out like the foul turds they are ... Show no mercy." Heydrich stood smartly to attention and saluted, avoiding Himmler's dagger looks. The Führer rose and embraced him again. "I have complete faith in you as always, my loyal Reinhard."

Heydrich clicked his heels smartly, saluted again, and left the office with a spring in his step.

The Count was not very happy at having to move again so quickly, but he brightened at the prospect of living in a castle again, one that did not consist mostly of ruins. Also, Heydrich assured him the journey would be much shorter, and faster—the Germans built good roads. They had all feasted well, so there was not too much grumbling from the 'girls' either. Their lust had returned with the fresh blood.

They had spent an enjoyable night together fulfilling mutual sexual needs—a trait inherited from their "living days". The Count had joined in for a brief while, but their exuberance had soon tired him. He sat, smoking one of his long cheroots and sipping a delicious vintage cognac as he watched the 'girls' exploring all manner of tested, and yet untested, means of satisfying each other with probing tongues and fingers until they were a mass of writhing flesh, indistinguishable, one from the other. The air filled with the sharp musk of wet female genitalia. It spread in waves like the breeze from a many, scented wild garden. Every fresh wave of the heavy, sex-drenched miasma urged deeper penetration. Their boundless enthusiasm and imagination, even after all the years they had spent together, never ceased to amaze him. He had to remember to buy some incense; perhaps patchouli would suit. The smell of this orgy would linger for hours, but the stains on his expensive rugs would remain forever. A shame ...

The Count was reminded, wistfully, of some of the orgies of ancient Rome, especially those held by the beautiful boy-emperor Caligula—whom he had once even thought of turning. But the tides of history were already lapping at Caligula's little boots. He would have been fun to have around at such moments, the Count thought, as he lit another cheroot and enjoyed the show. Caligula had been much more of an artist in the use human flesh than what he had seen of Hitler's pitiful daubs.

Heydrich had taken the trouble, no doubt out of his misplaced Nazi pride, to introduce the Count to a gentleman named Speer, who had shown him the grandiose designs of Hitler's proposed new Berlin. They really did remind him of Rome—but not in a good way.

CHAPTER FOUR

HEYDRICH, THE BUTCHER OF PRAGUE

He who fights with monsters might take care lest he thereby become a monster. And if you gaze for long into an abyss, the abyss gazes also into you.

Friedich Nietzche

Stellvertretender Reichsprotektor Reinhard Heydrich installed himself in his new Gestapo headquarters in the center of Prague. The news of his unwelcome arrival had spread through the newly created Protectorate of Bohemia and Moravia fast—as fast as it took to sign a Nazi death warrant. It was a grim forecast of things to come. He was rumored to be merciless beyond measure, and it was said that even his own SS Sturmtruppen feared him like no other general.

Heydrich's first orders arrived on the third day. They were concise, and bore Himmler's pragmatic trademark much more than Hitler's vague proposals. The Führer much preferred issuing his orders in person rather than writing them, and they were liable to change at any given moment. It kept the General Staff in a state of constant confusion. In his own way, Heydrich was very glad to be out of Berlin and it's ever-shifting politics.

According to the orders, there were the beginnings of an insurgency movement in Prague led by Jews, Marxists, and other Czech dissidents. Heydrich was all too aware of Himmler's and, in particular, Hitler's loathing of the Jews—so that came as no surprise. He shared that hatred. But what would have surprised him was that there was a Jew amongst the conspirators—they were too busy being exterminated by his colleague SS-Obersturmbannführer Eichmann. The Gestapo had obtained information on the locations and times of their meetings. It was to be passed on to the Count. The vampires were to be given SS uniforms with officer rank. They were to leave no one alive.

Heydrich visited the Count in his now more opulent surroundings in the Panenske Brezany Castle to convey the information in person. The Count declined any military rank, but told him to furnish his 'girls' with appropriate ones. They would be very particular about the tailoring, he told him. He gave him all their measurements from memory, and the appropriate ranks they should hold. It meant nothing to him, uniform or ranks, but the 'girls' did like their clothes. They would have to be made to measure, or they would refuse to wear them. Heydrich, with a certain amount of pride, informed him that the SS had their own bespoke tailor—a Mr Hugo Boss. He was already on his way.

"Remember, Count, no one must be left alive."

The Count nodded.

Herr Hugo Boss was nearly sixty years old, and in all his years of tailoring, he had never experienced anything remotely like what he was about to, except, perhaps, in his dreams. The women arrived at night to have their measurements taken. They were incredibly beautiful and exuded a heady sensuality that made his hands tremble. They trembled even more when the women unabashedly stripped off and stood unashamedly naked before him. He asked the Angelique woman if they could cover their modesty in some way. The woman laughed in his face. They wanted the clothes to fit exactly, and they wanted lingerie to match. Angelique also made a strange request: she wanted sewing kits for when they "changed," as she put it.

"Ach, I see ... You mean when you get pregnant," he said.

The women seemed to find this highly amusing. "Not exactly," Angelique said, "but they may get damaged in the course of our *work* ... We would like to be able to make our own repairs."

"Of course, madam, of course," Hugo said, nodding his head enthusiastically. He found he could not stop nodding. It was as if he had no control over his limbs. He tried to avert his eyes from the surrounding pubes. But it was impossible. They were practically thrusting their gorgeous cunts in his face. Their rich, perfumed aroma overwhelmed him. He felt he could bask in it forever. Much to his surprise, and immense embarrassment, he got an erection, something that had not happened for many years. The women giggled amongst themselves and seemed to deliberately rub their perfect buttocks and breasts against him at every opportunity. He felt like he was going to cum ... and he tried desperately to concentrate on his work. It was the hardest thing he had ever done. At last, the measuring was completed, and the women dressed and left. Hugo Boss immediately masturbated into one of his designer handkerchiefs. He had never ejaculated so much in his life, even in his younger years. His handkerchief was a sodden mess, and he had to throw it away. He worked all night, and the next morning, with the aid of half a dozen Pervitin—an indispensable aid when working for the SS, who expected everything to be done as speedily as possible. The consignment was ready for the mysterious women by midday. He so, so, wanted to please them, but much to his disappointment, he never saw them again. He was never to know how lucky he was ...

The vampires, freshly attired in their new uniforms, were accompanied by some Waffen SS soldiers from the notorious *Dirlewanger Brigade*, composed almost entirely of murderers and criminals. They had infamously burned women and children alive or fed them to their dogs. They were indifferent to killing and had participated in the first tentative mass extermination plans for the Jews—a task for which they were ideally suited. It was their fearsome reputation that had led Heydrich to assume they would be impervious to the horror of the vampires. He was wrong ...

There was one surviving soldier after the raid. He had turned into a blubbering wreck and was declared insane by the military medic. But he was not mad. Only Heydrich knew that. He interviewed him personally in a makeshift padded cell. The man was curled in a corner covered in his own excrement and vomit. Gradually, through many long hours of persuasive and gentle questioning (a first for Heydrich), he garnered the details of what had happened on that night.

Initially, the SS soldiers had been very disconcerted to find themselves accompanied by beautiful, female SS officers. But they found that the women were charming in their manner and carried their authority well, although many were planning to rape them if they could get the chance. They had been ordered to accompany the women, and no-one disobeyed orders issued by the Obergruppenführer— they knew too well the consequences. They did naturally wonder of what possible use the women would be when it came to the actual slaughter of the insurgents. This was their specialist field—not suited to delicate female eyes, even if those eyes did belong to SS officers.

The Gestapo's information had been correct, which was not unusual for them. The soldiers swiftly rounded up the ringleaders. The women seemed to bewitch the insurgents. They surrendered without a fight. The soldiers took them to an outlying wood to perform the executions, away from prying eyes and possible war crime witnesses. It should have been quick, but for some reason, their weapons were not functioning. The Feldwebel ordered them to use their daggers instead, but as they started to go about their business the females SS officers had fallen, snarling, upon the captives like hungered tigers and ripped them limb from limb. The soldiers found that every movement they made after that was like swimming through thick treacle as they watched the carnage unfold.

When they had finished with the captives, the vampires turned on them. The carnage was even worse. One of the monsters pinned him to the ground. Her jaw was horribly distended and too full of teeth, like an overloaded wolf's muzzle. He had heard about such things ... rumors ... legends ... as a child growing up in the Ukraine, but legends could be real—as real as blood. She/it seemed ready to tear his throat out. For some reason, she looked him in the eyes, which by that time were filled with tears. He never cried. He swore it. He was a soldier and was trained to kill. He had seen death in every form, but he had never dreamed of anything like this. Not even in his worst nightmares. But the wolf thing turned back into the major. She smiled and kissed him tenderly on the cheek like she were kissing a weeping child.

She had whispered in his ear, "I am Angelique," and then he had found he had the powers of his limbs again, and he had run and run from that terrible scene. He had run as if he could run forever, but he had known he would never escape.

Now he was here, and all he wanted was to die, but the doctors would not let him. He begged the Obergruppenführer to forgive his cowardice and give him a merciful death. He no longer wanted to exist in this world. This was not his world. This was a hell full of demons set on tormenting him.

Heydrich left the cell, and ordered the soldier's immediate execution. He was a danger to morale. Klein, Heydrich's chauffer, drove him speedily to the upper castle at Panenske Brezany just outside Prague—the temporary home of the vampires (Heydrich himself had decided to live in the lower castle so he could keep an eye on them). The Count was as polite and courteous as ever. His relaxed manner infuriated Heydrich. He dispensed with polite formalities.

"Why did you do it?" He could barely contain the raging fury that was bubbling up inside, threatening to engulf him. He was actually trembling with indignation as the Count took a deliberately slow sip of cognac from an extravagantly large balloon glass.

"My dear Heydrich, we followed your orders to the letter. "No one must be left alive"—they were your exact words, I believe." The Count raised his eyebrows. "It has come to my attention that unfortunately someone was spared. That's Angelique for you—she sometimes has her *human* moments still. Perhaps that's why I care for her ... " He sighed. "But I understand you have disposed of him, so all is well, is it not?" The Count offered Heydrich a cigar, which he declined with a fierce shake of his head. "Pity, they are very good. There is a fine tobacconist in the "Old

Town". It's just off Havelská Street ... You really must try it."

"Stop your inane ramblings!" Heydrich shouted. The Count's eyebrows shot up once again. "All is far from well, Count ... whatever your fucking name is ... I did not mean for you to kill our men as well. You knew that!"

"Oh, I'm sorry ... . You really should have been more explicit. We merely carried out what you ordered. As I recall telling you. I am a man of my word."

Heydrich, for once, found himself at a loss for words. There was nothing more to say except to utter all the expletives he could think of at the unruffled, abominable creature that sat before him. It was like spitting in the wind. He mustered whatever dignity he had left and marched out of the castle.

When he got back to his office, he lay his head on the desk. It was as heavy as lead. He felt like thumping it against the wood until he lost consciousness. He knew deep inside that his problems had only just begun. He was trapped in a nightmare from which there was no awakening.

CHAPTER FIVE

OPERATION SEALION

*The supreme art of war is to subdue the enemy
without fighting.*

Sun Tzu

The SS guard beat his arms together to keep
some circulation flowing even though he was wearing
a huge overcoat. It was the early hours of the morning
and it was freezing cold. It always seemed colder,
though, when you were guarding the SS Gestapo
Headquarters in Prague, even more so when the
Butcher, SS-Obergruppenführer Reinhard Heydrich,
was in residence. The guard gave a nervous glance up
at the General der Polizei's apartment. A dim light
glowed dully behind the heavy curtains. It never went
out, and the curtains were never drawn. Through a
small gap in the black velvet drapes, the guard could
just make out spindly, flickering shadows cast onto

the office's ceiling like cobwebs twitching with the death spasms of captured prey. It was rumored amongst his personal bodyguards that Heydrich conferred with Lucifer himself during the early hours. However ridiculous the gossip appeared during the cold light of day, in the early hours of the morning, it seemed almost plausible. Even the battle-hardened guard could not suppress a slight shudder. At times like these, he'd rather be back at the Eastern Front. At least there, you knew where the danger lay—however bad.

He marched back to the sentry hut, a temporary reprieve from the freezing wind. He was only allowed five minutes of standing time in the hut, and then he had to march one hundred meters and change to his counterpart's hut. Something fluttered past his face. It was too big to be a moth, probably a bat, too stupid to stay somewhere warm. Five minutes later, he stomped his feet and started his march back to the opposite hut. It wasn't until he was quite close to the sentry post that he noticed something wrong about his comrade. Unlike him, he was not encircled by white clouds of exhaled breath. His opposite number stood ramrod straight, but his skin was strangely etiolated—even his lips were gray. The guard peered under the man's helmet. He definitely wasn't breathing. He poked him experimentally in the ribs. The man fell quietly back into the sentry box, still stiffly at attention, like a wooden mannequin. The guard crossed himself, though as a member of the SS, he had forsaken religion, but old habits die hard. He had seen some strange sights during his years of service, but he had never actually seen someone die and remain standing. It was as though the soldier had become petrified, like some kind of vertical human fossil.

There was a discrete cough behind him. He whirled around to face the potential adversary, readying his rifle. When he saw who it was he quickly changed his aggressive posture into a submissive salute.

"What's going on here, Private?"

The guard swallowed hard. He hated addressing the person in front of him. It always felt strange to speak to the female SS major, and such an incredibly voluptuous one at that. But before the words had escaped his lips, the major had sunk her teeth into the pulsating vein in his throat and drained him as dry as his comrade.

SS-Obergruppenführer Heydrich paced the floor of his office with enough pent-up anger to wear holes in the carpet. The Count eyed him through his round, cerulean sunglasses with barely contained boredom.

"I thought we had an agreement ... We would supply you with human flesh, but on the condition that it was the flesh of our enemies. You have a whole ghetto of Jews for your brood to feast upon ... yet they have taken the lives of perfectly good soldiers of the Wehrmacht—yet again!"

"I am afraid your Jews provide very poor fare, my dear Heydrich. They are starved things ... more dead than alive. Their blood is very thin. It would barely pass as consommé ... You cannot blame my 'girls' for the occasional temptation."

"Do you mean to tell me you can't control your concubines, Count?"

"I should have explained something, General ... I really don't have much control over my consorts' blood lust, nor indeed their other *physical* lusts."

"They're your wives, aren't they, Count? Are you not the master of your own house? A good German wife would never think of conducting herself in such a disgusting ... wanton ... manner—it's indecent!"

"Alas, no, General, and may I say what an altogether gratifyingly erudite view of Teutonic sexual relationships. I'm almost tempted to don lederhosen and slap my knees."

Heydrich ignored the inherent sarcasm, or perhaps he didn't even recognize it as sarcasm. No one had ever dared to be sarcastic to him.

"Maybe in my younger days, I could have satisfied them and even had some measure of control over them ... but you see, I am old and feeble as far as they are concerned ... even though I am many times stronger than a mere mortal ... and you see my blood pressure is not what it used to be ... so they find solace with or *in* each other, you might say. But then their inclinations were always thus."

Heydrich grimaced. It was all so disgusting ....

"You mean to say they are lesbians as well as vampires ...? They are a disgrace to the SS uniform! What unholy brood have you unleashed on the city of Prague, Count?"

"We have just done what you asked, mein General—remember, it was you who came looking for us. You disturbed our slumber ... awakened once again our thirst for blood. But I do sympathize with your plight, believe me ... I will see what I can do. Perhaps, you could arrange for them to be smuggled into Great Britain. A relative of mine had some success there before, I believe."

Heydrich put his finger-tips to his temples as if he were suffering from a headache (a typical gesture when he was deep in thought), and pondered for a while. He was, in fact, trying to keep the Count's probing mind out of his. He was recalling an audience with the Fuhrer and Himmler only some days earlier:

He took one last critical glance at himself in the hallway, but he could find no fault in his always immaculate appearance. He raised his chin slightly higher in satisfaction. It was not just only out of personal vanity that he was so critical of his appearance, Heydrich, had always been a ladies man, and he knew that his smart, Boss, custom-tailored dark-black SS uniform was a guaranteed entrance to many a fräulein's bed, especially Nazi ones. His chauffeur, Klein, was on time and also smartly turned out, as always. He knew better than not to be. Heydrich was a stickler for discipline, and his punishments were severe, but Klein had been his chauffer for many years—he knew how to stay on the right side of his commander.

Today, Heydrich, wanted to make sure he was looking extra good, even beyond his normal strict parameters. He had a private meeting scheduled with Reichsführer Heinrich Himmler, his direct superior, and the Führer himself. His wife, Lina, was snoring peacefully, so he decided not to wake her. She was used to the odd hours he kept. He had some inkling of what the meeting concerned—the dead Waffen SS soldiers. The first unfortunate victims of the vampires.

The Führer had always held a deep reverence for Germanic mythology and, especially of late, an interest in the occult fired by the newly discovered vampires. Himmler had been insidiously encouraging his Führer's interest in the black arts, but Hitler was having trouble reconciling the cryptids with his long-held ideal of the Aryan race. The Reichsführer reasoned with him that knowledge of the black arts would aid them in their war against the Allies. Himmler, was a founding member of secret societies that the Führer was not even aware of, and if he had been, he would not have approved of many of them. But he was gradually letting himself be persuaded by Himmler's arguments. The slaughter of the soldiers both in Transylvania and now in Prague had undermined the Reichsführer's position, so he was shifting the blame onto Heydrich. The new Obergruppenführer had simply handled the vampires clumsily he told Hitler. When you are in possession of a new weapon you must first know how to use it lest you have accidents. Hitler did not think much of the accidents.

Heydrich arrived at the meeting in Himmler's office punctually .He was met with a cool greeting from the Reichsführer and a disconcertingly beaming welcome from the Führer—'Always, a pleasure to see you, Reinhard. How's Prague?'— which Heydrich found rather unsettling. There was definitely something in the air. The Führer's greeting might have been warm, but his eyes were deadly cold.

By the time he left the office, Heydrich had found that his suspicions had been fully justified. The Führer had somehow gotten it into his head (no doubt transplanted from Himmler's head), that the vampires would be better put to use as spies. There was a top-secret operation being planned for the invasion of Great Britain. Himmler handed him a thin brown dossier with the red Nazi Streng Geheim stamped on the Reichsadler. Below the Imperial Eagle, Heydrich, with a cursory glance, could just make out the title, 'Operation Sealion' written in traditional Gothic minuscule.

The vampires were to be deployed at his discretion, but henceforth, Heydrich was to take full responsibility for their actions. There were to be no more accidents ...

Heydrich had been wondering when he should mention that he intended to send them to Great Britain, and here was the Count, volunteering their services. It seemed too good to be true. Had the Count already known his intentions? There was no way of penetrating his inscrutable mask.

"They would certainly be far more useful to our cause there than here ... although ... smuggling coffins, let alone spies, into enemy territory will present difficulties," he said finally, as if he had been considering the Count's proposal at length.

"I am sure a man of your inestimable resources will be able to find a way. My concubines will be excited by the thought of fresh blood, and there will be many babies and healthy children, I think ... "

The Count made a great show of licking his thick lips greedily, as if savoring one himself. Heydrich shuddered at the sight—the Count seemed to delight in discomforting him.

"However," the Count added, "if you do manage to find a way, I will ... regrettably ... have to remain here. I'm too old for so much travel ... and I'm comfortable enough at the castle."

Heydrich nodded. Why wouldn't the Count be comfortable? He had lavish apartments in which to pass his waking hours and fresh victims, including virgins (his favorite), when they could find them. It was somewhat difficult finding unplucked cherries in Prague during the occupation. Every able-bodied girl was looking for some extra money for her household. The girls, and sometimes boys, got younger every day, but the old pervert didn't complain. No, the Count didn't have to lift a finger for his sick wishes to be fulfilled. But, on the other hand, his unusual services had repaid the Reich's generosity tenfold. The superstitious terror the vampires had now induced in the enemy was such that many of the battles were won even before they were fought. It was rumored that Allied soldiers in the trenches would drop their weapons at the mere mention of the monsters.

"We will find a way if there is one, Count. Of that, you may be assured. In the meantime ... would you be so kind as to talk to your major about my men? Killing any German soldier is bad enough ... but an SS soldier has the purest Aryan blood running through his veins—they are the future of the Fatherland." Heydrich, stood, clicked his boots together and gave an immaculate Nazi salute.

"Heil Hitler," Heydrich said, apparently with genuine enthusiasm. It marked the end of the meeting.

No wonder Heydrich was Hitler's favorite, the Count thought as he made to go. He, better than anyone, knew that a despot always needs his fanatics. He gave a lethargic attempt at a salute, as if waving away an irritating insect, and mumbled something hardly discernible. He strolled leisurely out of the SS-Obergruppenführer's office.

Heydrich sat back down behind his desk, furiously staring at the departing vampire's back. The Count somehow always managed to make him feel as though he was doing exactly as he pleased and Heydrich was his minion. His insolence was insupportable. But Heydrich had plans of his own for the Count and his 'girls'.

Later that night, the Count lay back on the chaise lounge, an exquisite example of its kind, looted from the palace of Versailles over two centuries ago by one of his minions when Louis XIV's back was turned. He was leisurely smoking an opium pipe while Angelique (a.k.a. Major von Rekowski) gently stroked his forehead with her cool hand. Sometimes, the pure, marblelike quality and coolness of her fine fingertips reminded him of her incomparable mother, Carmilla, and their times together in Venice. Carmilla had loved him deeply but had never really wanted to turn, never wanted her incomparable beauty to continue to exist unblemished through the ages. She had preferred the day to the night and had been content with the one passing into the other. Yet strangely, the Count had intuited, she had unconsciously wanted that dark, immortal life for her daughter. A strange preference.

He and Angelique had talked and made love, drifting aimlessly along the canals of Venice, during the long sunset hours. The red sky was reflected in the serene canals and seemed to turn them, appropriately, into rivers of blood.

"You really will have to desist from feasting on the SS men, my princess. The general is really becoming quite tiresome about it. After all ... you are meant to be one of their commanding officers. It simply won't do ... not good form. However much we may deplore their primitive politics, we owe them our resurrection ... even if they did it in ignorance."

Angelique, smiled wistfully.

"I often wonder if the SS might not be better off without the Obergruppenführer altogether ... he's far too fanatical, you know. It will only lead to ruin." She paused in her stroking. "And this thing with the Jews ... we owe them just as many favors as the SS. They did deny that accursed Christ person for us, didn't they?" The Count kept his own council and did not reply. Angelique continued: "If they just kept them well fed, they'd have another army ... and we'd have decent food. Instead, it's like drinking rats" piss ... What do they expect?"

"I have a surprise for you, my lovely. The general has plans to ship you across the channel to Great Britain. What do you think about that? A country with a whole host of sexually frustrated women with their unguarded offspring ... On top of that, all those lovely English fogs and chilly nights to stalk in."

Angelique couldn't contain her excitement and pleasure at the news. She clapped her dainty hands.

"Splendid! Prague was beginning to depress me. It just feels so ... vanquished."

"Off you go, then, my pet, and inform the other girls to make ready."

Angelique got up.

"Thanks for the treat, darling," she said, wheeling a black, veiled perambulator ahead of her. It contained a plump, contentedly burbling baby. The Count wondered if they would fuss and mollycoddle it or feast on it. Probably a bit of both, he decided.

The 'girls' were assembled in their underground lair deep under the castle. Their darker-than-black SS uniforms, designed personally for them by Herr Hugo Boss, were laid out neatly on the lids of their coffins. All they wore were their usual seductive silk stockings and suspenders, which they would have preferred to remain in, although they did like the sinister little death head's embroidered on their uniforms, and incidentally also on their lingerie. They all held officer's ranks, although Angelique, being the "oldest" had been given the highest.

They crowded around the only mirror in the dungeon, applying their make-up, giggling as they made pouting shapes with their mouths to apply lipstick or surprised looks with their eyebrows while they applied eyeliner. It was a very beautiful gilded mirror in the most exquisite taste, as were all the rest of the furnishings that had been transported directly from the Count's castle in Transylvania. It was also a very special mirror. It was one of a pair that had belonged to Vlad the Impaler, the only known mirrors to successfully reflect vampires. They did not, however, reflect human beings. Many decades ago, they had led the unfortunate and already slightly demented Jonathan Harker to believe that he was turning into a vampire. It had tipped his befuddled brain over the edge. His fragile mind had been finally broken by those great, mysterious mirrors.

Angelique had told the other five vampires of the impending trip to England, and they were all just as excited as she was. The news had even brought a slight flush to all their normally pallid but pristine features, and none of them needed so much rouge that evening. Dorotea Fanshaw, a young (turned young by Angelique) Englishwoman, was trying to breastfeed the baby. But her teats only leaked blood, which she was upset to find the baby did not seem to like. She would have to purloin some cow or human milk—

disgusting stuff that it was. She dry heaved at the thought. Being, female SS officers, none of them should have been wearing makeup, but no one of whatever rank in the SS would have ever pointed the indiscretion out. The members of Heydrich's special vampire unit were a law unto themselves. Even without the SS-Obergruppenführer's blessing, it was doubtful that any man alive could have withstood their sexual charms, not to mention their fatal ones.

Only one of the vampires, Selene, a sultry West Indian beauty, had some regrets about leaving. She had a young, ardent lover amongst the Czech underground. A man named Stef who had unwittingly revealed the names of many of his comrades in the resistance whilst under Selene's hypnotic charms. He was a magnificent, greedy lover whose sexual appetite nearly matched hers—only nearly, though. To have matched it would have been impossible for any mortal. In the throes of his orgasms, which Selene purposefully prolonged into the most exquisite torture, she would feast on a little of his pulsating blood. Her favorite way of feasting she had found lately was to take him in her mouth and, as his member had its huge spasms of egress, suck blood along with his jism. Tonight, she would have to drain him of both. Her delicate, snake-like tongue whipped out and touched her top lip in anticipation and her eye teeth lengthened and grew sharper. She would try to be gentle with him. He deserved that much, at least, for the pleasure he had given her.

The 'girls' helped each other dress. This was their favorite part of the evening. Freshly awoken, comfortable in the warm depths of their long comradeship, yet feeling the first pangs of the red hunger ... it was a good time. They caressed and fondled each other. With warm, intimate embraces, murmuring, gasping, and sighing, they satisfied at least one passion before they embarked on the night's adventures. Each of them had their separate plans for the evening. They seldom worked in pairs.

Not all their plans coincided with the Nazi war effort. The vampires considered the politics of war trivial. The only advantage for them was that there was a lot more killing going on than there would be in peace time, and under the throes of the Third Reich, there was a lot of killing indeed. It meant that their sanguinary exploits went virtually unnoticed. What were a few more corpses compared to the thousands dying every day? And in the case of the Nazis, they were actively endorsed. The vampires made great spies, gathering information that mortals could not, and they were natural killing machines.

Heydrich was anything if not efficacious. The removal of the vampires to Great Britain was immediately put into effect. The 'girls' were naturally disappointed that the Count would not be accompanying them, but it also had its advantages insofar as they would have more freedom. However, Angelique had impressed on them the Count's strong telepathic powers, and it would not do to become overly incautious. He was and always would be their master, and not just by choice.

Selene had done for her lover, and now Dorotea had to do for the baby. She had grown quite attached to the little thing, a strange sensation for a vampire, who usually only perceived mortals as food. Angelique allowed her the first bite ....

The coffins were smuggled ashore from a U-Boat off England's south-eastern coast, and from there to the house of a German collaborator by means of a labyrinth of underground tunnels that laced the chalky foundations of all those seaside towns and villages, dating back to when they had been the haunts of smugglers.

Mr. Baker (the pseudonym Herr Schultz had adopted many years ago) had been warned that these were no ordinary soldiers slumbering in the coffins and he was to leave two live human beings locked in the room with the coffins and he was to turn a deaf ear to any noises he might hear.

Schultz had long ago ceased to impugn the increasingly preternatural orders of the Third Reich. He managed to persuade two of the local vagabonds, with the aid of a bottle of whisky and the promise of more to come, to stand vigil over the coffins inside a locked room in his cottage.

The screams were terrible. It was lucky his house stood alone on a heath far away from the village. They eventually subsided. After a while, there was a knock on the room's locked door.

"You may let us out now," an unmistakably husky female voice said.

Schultz had not been told there would be women. His lasciviousness nearly got the better of him, but common sense prevailed. What kind of women would be witness to whatever massacre had taken place behind the heavy door?

He opened it only to find a smiling, simply yet elegantly dressed Angelique. She strolled past him as he were not there. So did five other women. Their beauty made his 'Heil Hitler' clog in his throat. He could just make out the inside of the room they had vacated. It looked like a wild beast had been set loose. With the amount of unidentifiable flesh scattered around, it should have smelled like a charnel house, but surprisingly, there was no trace of blood, just the unmistakable tang of vacated bowels.

He was about to protest about all the cleaning up he would have to do and ask where the male officers were when Angelique softly placed a finger on his lips as if reading his thoughts

"Best not to ask," she said. "Just dispose of the mess."

He went to fetch a shovel, mop, and bucket. The mysterious woman's touch had been enough for him to know that he would do well to obey, and he was so eager to do so. After he had finished cleaning up the macabre scene he turned back to the woman, longing for her acknowledgement of his hard work. Angelique and the others were all huddled over a map. She seemed to sense his imploring look and glanced up briefly in the direction of the room. It was as if she could see inside without even moving. She nodded her silent approval. His heart skipped a beat at this small sign. If this was the kind of women the Fatherland was producing, what would the real soldiers be like when the invasion started ...?

"Thank Gott ... The war will soon be over and we will reign supreme," he said with the hope of more approval.   Angelique put her head to one side and raised an eyebrow quizzically. She seemed genuinely perplexed by Schultz's patriotic statement.

"Why on Earth would we want that?" she said and gave him another of her radiant smiles. "Come here."

He approached the table like a dog expecting a treat. All he lacked was the lolling tongue and wagging tail.

"You need to lay the table for lunch," she "I will see right to it right away. I don't have much ... just poor village fare, I'm afraid ... what with all the rationing ... and whatnot."

He made to go. One of the women pulled him back. She was surprisingly strong.

"Oh, silly me," Angelique said, putting her hand coquettishly to her mouth." I should have said *lie* on the table for lunch."

"What ...?"

He still didn't understand. Not until they picked him up as if he were a feather, hurtled him onto the rough wood, and commenced ripping his body apart. Then he understood, and his terrible screams echoed the depth of his understanding.

CHAPTER SIX

RIDE OF THE VALKYRIES

*Revenge, the sweetest morsel to the mouth that
ever was cooked in hell.*

Walter Scott—The Heart of Mid-Lothian

SS Major von Rekowski (aka Angelique Carmilla
Agoult d'Archambault) was not happy. Their mission,
if it could be termed that, was not proving a success—
that is, according to German High Command. Her
'girls' were enjoying the easy pickings amongst
temporarily abandoned housewives, war widows, and
their children, but they had also been faithful to their
mission. She could find no fault with them there.
They had managed to remain relatively inconspicuous
by limiting their feasting to a few households in every
village. For the vampires, the children were the
sweetest meats, their blood rich with energy and
innocence. They curbed their feeding frenzies so as

not to arouse suspicion, and concentrated for the most part on the evacuee children. Meanwhile, they spied and gathered information in accordance with their orders. The evacuees' foster parents were not particularly upset by the rise in deaths of the children in their care, nor were their parish councils. They put it down to anemia and the undoubtedly unhealthy, squalid conditions the children had endured in the metropolis. When all was said and done, they were not their children. Taking care of a lot of these war refugees was considered nothing but a semi-imposed patriotic duty and, at the same time, a drain on thrift-conscious households. Patriotic duty stretched only as far as purse strings.

Angelique held the letter from SS-Obergruppenführer Heydrich at arm's length, as if it had been written on freshly soiled toilet paper. They were being recalled only a few months into their mission. Evidently, the Obergruppenführer was not pleased with their results and believed their special skills could be used more effectively elsewhere—like the Russian front. It would mean soldiers' blood again, full of fear, rage and doubt, not the rich fare they had become accustomed to. She had had to recall her sisters in darkness from their various hidden lairs scattered around Kent and the Home counties via a mind call. They were to meet at their original landing site to await evacuation.

As far as Angelique was concerned, their tight-knit brood had done exceptionally well considering the circumstances. It had proven remarkably difficult to remain incognito in England. They had to spend a large part of their waking hours in various disguises and hiding places. The British were remarkably paranoid about outsiders. She thought they had every right to be; after all, they were a country at war. Much as the vampires tried to disguise their inherent foreignness there was no disguising the fact that to most Englishwomen, they were sexual predators: exotic, extremely attractive in their very foreignness, and, no doubt, intent on seducing the very few viable men left in the country. Therefore, they were considered competitors, except, in rare cases, by those open-minded women that had realized the women's true sexual nature. These tribade women shared many nights of proscribed bliss with them before their inevitable demise.

The reaction of the general populace had forced them into being furtive—inherently against their nature. It was only Angelique, who was French and, therefore considered a kind of ally, and Dorotea Fanshaw, a well-brought-up young English lady, who were relatively tolerated by the women. The men, on the other hand, fawned over them. It was because of this that the two vampires had managed to penetrate the upper spheres of the English political and military hierarchy. Their task was not so much to assassinate, but to gain information.

Angelique had decided that she would seduce Churchill, but the bulldog-like prime minister had proven as stoic as his reputation. She had found it impossible to penetrate the great man's thoughts, which mostly, on the surface, seemed to revolve around brandy, cigars, painting mediocre watercolors, and infuriating Hitler. She had not expected such a strong mind-probe defense from a mere mortal. It was as if his thoughts really did consist of such idiocies, but of course, that would be impossible—he was Britain's war leader.

SS-Obergruppenführer Heydrich, compared to the Axis and Allied figureheads, tended to look at things pragmatically, logically even, as far as was humanly possible given the highly unusual circumstances he found himself in. He considered himself something of a philosopher along Greek lines, with a Spartan disposition and temper that did not admit contradiction. He had decided some time ago that the vampires were becoming a liability in terms of their worth. He wanted to dispose of them, but he was very wary of the dark powers the Count commanded. He knew from brutal experience how powerful that immortal being was. He still hadn't managed to erase from his memory that terrible night when they had awakened the vampires—the way the Count had paralyzed his body and so easily penetrated his mind. He knew he could not afford to openly be the Count's enemy. He would have to find more subtle methods to undermine the Nosferatu's power, and he had to make sure that whatever he did remained in the background, unseen and unheard. He would rely on the soldier's well-worn excuse: "Just following orders," however vague they might be.

He had therefore decided to send the 'girls' on a far riskier operation, and if they should die (this time for good), he could not be held responsible. He was sure their deaths would weaken the Count's resolve to a degree in which he could take suitable advantage—even a vampire must feel some remorse. He would provide solace for the Count in whatever way he could. He would become the Nosferatu's willing apprentice, discover the dark secrets he craved, even, perhaps, persuade the Count to *turn* him—he would surely feel lonely enough to crave a companion-in-darkness, and who better than the man who had revived him?

The Count had warned him once, in one of their less argumentative conversations, about gaining the sort of knowledge he wanted. "You humans have a saying ... I believe, it goes: 'Seek and you shall find ...' but, I will tell you this ... Be very sure about what you want to know ... because once you pass through that doorway into the *hidden* reality, it will shut behind you as surely as a nailed coffin lid."

The Count's dire warnings did not trouble Heydrich in the least. He was sure he could make much better use of the powers bestowed upon an immortal—immortality was his fate. A man like him should never have to die. He was determined never to become a mere footnote in history books. He would be history itself. His longings were not restricted to mere mental and physical power. He also craved the Count's possessions. A man was not only judged by the power he wielded, but also by his riches, and some things were worth more than mere currency. Things that mere mortals could only covet.

The Count could have told him that he should be more worried about Angelique than trying to gain his dark powers, but most humans held little interest for him, and Heydrich even less. He had met his kind countless times. Angelique was angry, and an angry Angelique was a far ... from .. ,.pleasant proposition. Her dislike for Heydrich and what he represented had turned to hatred. In Angelique's case this was nearly always fatal.

Unfortunately for Heydrich, the feeling was not entirely mutual. He could not help himself. He felt unnaturally attracted to the vampire, and as much as he tried to suppress the unwanted feeling, it would not leave him. It was like a personal disease that he could not and would not admit to, even to himself. He could still remember that terrible night when she had changed into a monster in human form. Nevertheless, he still felt a perverted sexual attraction to her. Maybe he saw the monster inside himself in female form, and he loved his monster. What was worse, he was sure she knew it. Her remarks to him were often flirtatious invitations, but he had to admit to himself that he was too deeply scared of her to flirt back. It was shameful. Sometimes, the sexual attraction would overwhelm him, and it took all his iron will power to restrain himself from falling into those arms, which he was sure would embrace him ... The heady thought of what lay between those wonderful alabaster legs ... how they would open to him. His frustration meant that many nights, he lost himself in the local brothels, taking whore after whore until his need was satiated. He dreaded the nights she came to him for orders ... that provocative slight smile that played around her lips when she asked how he was, as if she didn't know ... how she always managed to leave him with an erection despite how much her insolence annoyed him.

The 'girls' were as disillusioned and annoyed by the news as much as Angelique. They agreed to her vengeful plan: they would indeed return to Germany to be debriefed prior to their new assignment, but before they left for Russia they would consign SS Obergruppenführer Heydrich to a living death.

The Count was finding his visits to the Obergruppenführer's office in Prague increasingly irritating. In fact, he was on the verge of losing his good manners, and to a gentleman like the Count, the prospect was abhorrent. The Obergruppenführer's latest outrage of accusing his 'girls' of not taking their work seriously, and his proposal to send them into the wastes of the Eastern Front were simply appalling. Vampires did not particularly like the cold, although, paradoxically they were cold personified. He'd even had the audacity to suggest that the Count might care to join them!

The SS Obergruppenführer did not even have the courtesy to invite him to sit once he had been ushered into his office by an indifferent SS guard. Heydrich waved his hand nonchalantly at him, pointing to a chair, while talking on the telephone. He had not even stood to greet him when the Count had entered. The immortal felt his ancient Nosferatu blood start to heat with annoyance. He felt his teeth lengthen. He bit his lower lip, savoring his own blood to stem his temper. The 'girls' could feel his anger as far away as England. Yet this rude mortal in his crude military uniform sensed nothing. In fact, this Heydrich, mistakenly believed that he was intimidating him. Him! The Count almost laughed out loud it was so preposterous.

He seated himself in the leather chair, placing his walking stick topped with its small ivory skull, set with rubies for eyes, carefully across his lap. The Obergruppenführer finished his conversation and put down the heavy black Bakelite telephone. He eyed the

Count's walking stick enviously. He had long coveted it. Heydrich coveted skull symbols, and he knew that it would make Himmler, who shared his mania, incredibly jealous—an added bonus. Even though he had dropped numerous hints that it would make a fine gift, the Count seemed immune to them. And he was much too proud to ask if he could have it. Heydrich had made up his mind that one day, he would have it—with or without the Count's consent. The Count, for his part, felt the tide of petty envy emanating from the human wash over him like a warm and welcome shower. He bathed in the delightful sin of it. It made him feel slightly less annoyed.

The Obergruppenführer coughed to clear his throat, and the Count raised his eyebrow. This was their usual prelude to a conversation now: neither one prepared to break the silence unless forced to. Finally, Heydrich gave way and said, "Good evening, Count. I trust you have slept well."

The Count replied equally politely, and with the formalities out of the way they could get down to the real business of moving him and his 'girls' to Russia. The Obergruppenführer made it abundantly clear that he would not change his mind over the matter of the vampires being moved to the Russian front. He even made a clumsy attempt at suggesting that in return for the Count's invaluable signature walking stick, he might delay the order for the Count to join them. The Count left the office (still with his walking stick) and still in a foul temper.

Angelique decided that before they took their leave of England they would have a night to remember. It was also to be a night of terror for the tiny village of Feathershore-on-Sea that would never be forgotten.

The vampires rampaged through the village, satiating their every lust. By the time sunrise arrived, every household in the hamlet had cause to lament. Death had visited every one. The manner of the deaths had striking resemblances in that all the victims appeared drained of blood, but their corpses had been ripped apart as if by a frenzied animal. Young women and children formed the majority of the gruesome deaths. If it had not been for the sighting of a German U-boat the next day, it would have been a top story in the London press. As it was, with the increasing threat of invasion from the Germans, along with the ever-present insidious threat of the U-boats, it hardly got a mention. By the time the war ended, the horrific events of that night had become a legend, a tale of huge bats, wolves and frenzied dogs attacking people and ripping their throats out, of pale women with bloodied ruby lips and cold eyes, passionately kissing dying women who writhed in pain and pleasure. It was a dark night of blood, fire, and according to the local vicar, brimstone.

Their blood lust well and truly satiated— for the time being— the vampires had taken to the skies and flew south to their original landing point. The Count had extended his power to them through Angelique so that they could fly for small distances in bat form. They sealed themselves inside their wooden caskets in Herr Schultz's old house, ready for the journey back to Germany. Even as her eyes grew heavy and closed of their own accord for the day's ritual slumber, Angelique was still plotting her revenge.

When they finally returned to their master, the Count was sitting amongst the packing crates containing his great works of art and priceless furniture. There was a cheerful fire crackling in the castle's huge fireplace, but it was not the spitting flames from the logs that warmed his ancient bones (they could never be physically warmed again): it was the great, dark love shared with his 'girls' that touched his sepulchered heart. The flames danced like the burning desire they had for one another. He realized with a shock that he was happy that they were back. It was an alien sensation. Most of the time he had spent with them in Prague, he had been sorting out the problems their killing sprees had caused. True to form, they had arrived on the back of another one.

The Count briefly rested his hand on top of the kneeling Angelique's head. It was almost like a benediction. In a way, it was. He had agreed on her planned course of action, although he would miss his brief sojourn amongst the living.

CHAPTER SEVEN

OPERATION ANTHROPOID

Pleasure in the job puts perfection in the work

Aristotle

Heydrich was in the bathroom, singing one of his favorite arias from Wagner—badly. His father had been a composer and opera singer, but Heydrich had not inherited his musical prowess. He did, however, know all the words to Wagner's operas. Indeed, his second name, Tristan, had been given to him in honor of Wagner's opera, *Tristan und Isolde*. Unbeknown to him, the moment would have been better suited to a rendition of the "Ride of the Valkyries," because, at that very moment Angelique and the girls were flying in his direction with terrible intent.

Heydrich was looking forward to his meeting with Hitler. The weather was clement, and he was to travel to Berlin in his favorite staff car: an open-top Mercedes. He was not afraid of assassination attempts, and he liked to demonstrate it. Who, after all, would dare to kill a demigod?

The car was slowing to take a bend on the road out of Prague when he sensed a presence beside him. He turned to find a serenely smiling Angelique sitting beside him. He was momentarily startled, losing his customary air of cool command in any situation. His eyes widened in surprise. Then, regaining his composure, he was merely perplexed. Why couldn't his driver, Klein, see her? Then he remembered there would be no reflection in the mirror, but still, the question remained: how was it possible she was here in daylight? Was he hallucinating? And why couldn't Klein at least hear her? His quick mind ran through a series of questions and explanations in seconds.

"He can't hear or see me because I am cloaked in invisibility," she said, as if reading his thoughts.

"What are you doing here in daylight? Isn't it fatal to your kind?" Heydrich meant to say it calmly, but it turned out more of a snarl, an unblendable mixture of hate and desire, and he hated himself for it—as always. "I have not given you permission for an audience. I only speak to the Count, your master. Get out of my sight!"

Angelique gave him that soft smile again, slightly revealing her pin-sharp canine teeth. Heydrich shuddered. She neglected to mention that the Count had bestowed upon them the gift of day-walking through his own psyche. It was one of many powers he could use when called upon. It wouldn't last long, but it would last long enough for Angelique to do what she planned to do.

Then Heydrich did something totally unexpected, as was his way—he laughed in her face! No man had ever dared to do that. Not even the Count when he was in high spirits. For a moment, she nearly forgot herself and her carefully laid plans. She stifled a snarl as she readied herself to rip his throat out. Instead, she found herself recoiling in horror and nausea as Heydrich proceeded to produce a dreaded object from around his neck. It was Vlad the Impaler's own silver crucifix before he had led his children to the dark side. It was the most powerful crucifix in the world, and its pain was unbearable to "young vampires"—those born after the birth of Christ. It's light burned her inside as if she had swallowed acid.

"You foolish young woman. Did you think I would have dared to awake the Count from his long sleep if I wasn't suitably armed? I would have been his first victim." He didn't tell her that much to his disappointment at the time, the Count had completely ignored it. He had made him feel like a child waving a water pistol. This time, much to his satisfaction, it was having the desired effect.

Heydrich hadn't taken into account the other vampires. Selene, seeing Angelique's predicament from their ambush site, launched a grenade. The fierce explosion rocked the heavy Mercedes and Heydrich loosened his grip on the crucifix. It was the chance Angelique needed. She struck his arm, breaking the chain holding it around his neck. It landed in the bushes by the side of the road. Heydrich was defenseless. Stripped of any pretense of control or power, he screamed in real fear and panic for the first time in his life. He sounded like a little girl—the most exquisite music to Angelique's ears.

She didn't waste any further time talking with the cursed wretch of a human. She took his head and bent him to her. He could not resist her steely embrace. She had the supernormal strength of the undead. In the final moment before she plunged those dainty fangs into his neck, Heydrich couldn't help thinking how stupid he had been to meddle with the powers of darkness in the first place. It was his ultimate acceptance of failure, the surrender of a drowning man as his lungs filled with the illimitable water of the ocean.

Angelique had reserved a very special kiss for Heydrich. This was not the normal kiss of death, where she would suck her victim dry. This kiss was a paralyzing osculation in which he would suffer the torments of hell for hundreds of years. She reached into his chest, squeezed his heart, and licked the blood daintily off her fingers, all while giving him the sweetest of her smiles. It was done in a moment—she had made him a living corpse.

The 'girls' placed the bodies at some distance from the car so it looked like Heydrich and Klein had been in the act of pursuing their assailants and collapsed from their wounds. Then they flew ...

The 'girls' had disguised themselves in Czech partisan uniforms and dispatched other German soldiers en route to make it look like the men had died in a firefight with partisans. To all intents and purposes, it would appear a human attack upon the SS Obergruppenführer's life. They had, of course, helped themselves to some of the pumping blood, and their barely living victims had watched in horror as they'd fallen upon their open wounds with relish, slicing with their razor teeth and probing with their snake like tongues for every precious drop of blood. The ferocity of those eyes, turned bright crimson with blood lust, would be the last thing the soldiers remembered of the mortal world as they thankfully left it.

SS Obergruppenführer Heydrich was in the hospital for a week. He was attended by the best Nazi doctors. He appeared to be alive but semi-paralyzed, sometimes at the point of recovery and sometimes lapsing into a coma. Finally, the foolish humans would think he was dead and would inter him. Angelique had even fashioned the features of his face, giving him a beatific and peaceful expression. She visited him once in his hospital bed in her bat form, flitting briefly in front of his face just to let him know she was there. If bats can't grin then she did a remarkable impression of one. No one could imagine the terrible suffering his soul was experiencing—alive and dead at the same time, aware of what was going on around him but unable to move or even utter a sound. He watched as the nurses with undisguised disgust cleaned his anus and bed sheets of the free-flowing, stinking excrement that constantly streamed from his bowels, the doctors mournfully shook their heads and shrug, and the surgeons pulled tiny pieces of cloth from his wound with pointed tweezers. He felt everything in excruciating detail.

Once interred, he would be at Angelique's mercy. And she would make sure he knew it. He would become the vampire's plaything, seemingly dead, but alive for her to commit terrible torment upon for centuries, even if all that remained of him was rotting flesh and bones. No creature, even in the depths of hell, would know such unutterable misery and pain. A lone tear coursed down his cheek and over the contours of his face. Time had no meaning in his new reality. The tear moved as slowly as a glacier meandering its course over a desolate landscape.

The high-ranking Nazis who knew of the vampires and their secret pact with Heydrich, were convinced that the vampires were responsible, although all evidence pointed to the contrary—the SS had arrested two Czech soldiers after a tip-off. Heinrich Himmler, Reichsführer of the Schutzstaffel, in particular, was convinced of the vampires" culpability. But the pact with the vampires had to be kept secret. The SS discovered more dead conspirators in a crypt bearing the trademark of the vampires" attacks: corpses shrunken and desiccated, papyrus-like skin (what was left of it) clinging to yellowed skeletons, puncture holes larger than even a tiger could inflict covering what was left of necks and chests, skulls caved in like rotten tomatoes, no sign of any blood, bits of flesh hanging from the ceiling and splattered on the walls ... They were declared suicides.

Himmler decided they must have a hidden lair in a village called Lidice. The Nazis spared no one and leveled the village to the ground in the hope of burning out the vampires.

They missed their chance, and all their vengeance was in vain. The Count and his 'girls' had returned to his impregnable crypt under the castle in the Urals to sleep once again the long sleep of the undead.

THE COUNT AND ANGELIQUE

While the vampires slept, the Count and Angelique dreamily chased the ghosts of their mutual past through the labyrinth of their shared days and eternal nights ...

Baronne Carmilla Archambault was accustomed to her solitary daughter's moods and whimsies, but this really was too much. Angelique had been refusing all her suitors for so long now that the baron and baronne had been contemplating physically forcing their willful offspring to marry. The baron was too weak to deal with her, and Angelique played him for a fool. Now, to add to her growing flagitiousness, the terrible child had contrived to let herself be caught in flagrante delicto with one of the housemaids! It would have been bad enough if it had been one of the valets, but at least it would have been *natural*.

News of the scandal had reached the very court itself. It had, evidently, according to what tittle-tattle you listened to, even given King Louis XIV some little amusement. The baronne was sure she would never be able to show her face in court again. Worse, no one would want to marry their daughter now even with her handsome dowry. To do so would mean becoming a laughing stock.

In fact, the only person who was most decidedly laughing at that moment was Angelique. She had considered the whole thing a delightful prank, one that she had personally contrived and pulled off. She had also discovered something of vital importance to herself, something she had suspected for a long time: she preferred the sexual pleasures of women to men. Losing herself between the sweaty thighs of the housemaid had been bliss, and when the young woman had expertly returned the favor, she'd thought she would scream with pleasure. There was so much to explore in a woman, unlike the simple, cheesy phalluses of most men she had entertained.

Things didn't end there, though. King Louis, always one to fly in the face of convention, invited Angelique to his court to be a lady-in-waiting to his wife, Maria Theresa of Spain. The baron and baronne could not believe their luck. At one stroke, they had rid themselves of their troublesome daughter and had their honor restored. There were unsubstantiated rumors that the whole episode with the housemaid had been a cleverly staged intrigué in order for the king to take an interest in Angelique—a perfectly contrived coup d'état, according to the gossips at court. It made them appear the most cunning and contriving of ambitious parents—a label they basked in. The baron and his wife did nothing to quell the rumors: in fact, they positively encouraged them. At their now numerous dinner parties, the baronne would, of course, publicly deny any such scheming, but she would occasionally bestow on her fawning audience a conspiratorial wink, fanning the flames of her now eminent reputation.

Her reputation as a prime manipulator brought her not only to the attention of other ambitious women, but also men, whom she took full advantage of. Carmilla was in her sexual prime, and coupled with her dazzling beauty she had no end of suitors. Her sexual appetite knew no bounds, and each man only temporarily satiated it. Sometimes, she would take two or three to her bed at once. The bed's semen-stained and sweat-soaked sheets were changed on a regular basis throughout the day by her giggling chamber maids. The Baron was quite aware of his wife's "indiscretions" and had long since given up trying to stop her. He knew better than to unleash his wife's venomous tongue on himself; much better that it was put to use licking a man's cock than castigating him. He preferred his books and fine wine collection. His favorite pastime was to indulge in both in his extensive library. It was so much more relaxing than mounting his wife and trying to maintain the ferocious gallop she demanded. He was secretly hoping that the numerous lovers would produce a male heir. It would be a bastard, but anything was better than leaving his large estate to his headstrong daughter. But his equally intransigent wife refused to bear any more children despite the floods of sperm that was constantly poured between her loins.

Angelique delighted the court and quickly became one of the king and queen's favorites. She possessed a keen intelligence, combined with a ready wit, and was always quick off the mark with an appropriate, amusing riposte. But she also had a rapier sharp tongue like her mother and had no hesitation in using it. She reserved her most venomous sarcasm, which could be very cruel, for would-be suitors. They would wither under the spite of her words and humiliating rejection. She enjoyed nothing more than luring a young man to her bed and then watching as his penis deflated under her scornful gaze. She wondered what her mother would make of such behavior. Her mother never let a hard cock go to waste. The only time she would allow one to wilt was when it had spent its seed inside her.

Even so, Angelique was not immune to the financial benefits of marriage, although she publicly feigned abhorrence of the institution. She already had her eyes on a spouse with a suitable title and financial means ...

Comte Agoult was nearly sixty years old and feeble. He really didn't know what to do when Angelique started to make her feelings clear; after all, she was notorious for her dislike of the opposite sex. Was it all some sort of an act, or was she really attracted to him? it was not unknown for younger women to be attracted to older men but it was usually for the wrong reasons. He did not know whether to be flattered or on guard. He had heard about her scheming mother, and the apple did not fall far from the tree. He did not consider himself stupid or naive and had no illusions about his physical appearance. He was more than old enough not to flatter himself. He was not in the slightest bit attractive, in fact; he was downright ugly. His nose was large and angular, and dominated his pinched features and tight lips, which, coupled with his thin moustache gave him a vulture-like appearance. An undernourished vulture. He was stooped, nearly completely bald, and covered already in a wealth of liver spots (hidden under so many layers of powder that a dusty cloud seemed to permanently orbit his features) because of his addiction to wine and port. He had no direct heirs, so it was clear to him the young woman was only after his title, money, and the power that went with both. On the other hand, was it not better to die happily between the legs of such a bewitching young creature than wallow in the steady decline towards senility?

And within a few weeks of their marriage, he did die. Whether the marriage was ever consummated, no one dared ask. It was a detail that Angelique was extremely reticent about. She said she would take that piece of information confidentielle with her to the grave. The comte, nevertheless, did die of a heart attack in bed with her. But there was no trace of a smile on his face. It was more a look of ultimate surprise.

After a while, the nefarious, whispered tittle-tattle ran itself dry .... She was now one of the most desirable women at court, and she took to her new social standing with obvious relish.

The new comtesse, Angelique Agoult d"Archambault, was more than happy with the spiteful court rumors. They kept nearly all but the most ardent of suitors of the recently widowed belle at bay. It also gave her ample opportunity to satisfy her own voracious sexual appetite in secret. She now took both male and female lovers, sometimes both together. She became a discrete seductress, a ferocious sexual predator with her carefully concealed arrière-pensée.

Then, one day, everything changed ... The king employed her as a spy. She did it purely for the thrill as she had no need of money. That was one of the reasons why the king trusted her, as was the fact she shared his sense of wicked mischievousness.

Baronne Archambault had, to everyone's surprise, not least the Baron's, stopped the steady stream of beaus sharing her bed and taken to late-night rendezvous with a mysterious stranger. The unknown, handsome Count had appeared out of nowhere in the city and, without preamble, presented himself to the baron and baronne, who could not help but be flattered by the unexpected attention. Try as they might, they could find out nothing about the mysterious Count in Paris or the rest of France. He seemed to be an enigma, as elusive as his whereabouts—no one even knew where he lodged in Paris. His black, ornate carriage appeared invariably at night at odd times and places. He exuded power and wealth, combined with effortless charm. The women at court were besotted.

He nearly always wore dark glasses. The gossips put this down to the recently discovered disease of photophobia—an intolerance of light— probably, an aristocratic heritage. Others, more mischievously, suggested it was a permanent hangover, although, the Count always drank in moderation and only the very best wine, in public, at least ... She had once been privileged to witness him remove his glasses to polish them. He had caught her stare and transfixed her with blazing black eyes that she was sure turned a crimson red, but she could not hold that blinding gaze for long.

The baronne was fascinated by him. He was tall, dark-haired, and always immaculately dressed. Carmilla's sexual antennas were quivering. There was something unique about this man, and she longed to possess him. She sensed a great power within him, a power that intrigued her but, at the same time repelled and frightened her. She yearned to know more of it. In private, she openly flirted with him. He seemed impervious to the carnal delights she was so eager to bestow upon him.

The Count travelled to Venice. Paris seemed dead and empty without him. The baronne followed him like a faithful lap dog, leaving her husband with his musty books. Their nights together passed as if in a blissful dream, at least for the baronne. The Count had finally fallen for her relentless advances. He proved to be the best lover she had ever had—she was finally satisfied. She had even managed to get him to reveal his family name: Dragwlya. But the Count steadfastly refuse to tell her his Christian name. He claimed, bizarrely, to have forgotten it.

Her suspicions about him started with that most common of human faults: jealousy. The Count would disappear for days on end without any kind of explanation. She had too much experience in dealing with men to let her feelings show. She toyed with the idea of having him followed. Venice was famous for its professional and, more importantly, discreet private spies. She had noticed that he was always strangely lethargic during the day. He had a habit of lying in bed most of the daylight hours with the curtains drawn. If he did venture out, it was always in the late afternoon, and he inevitably wore his round, dark-blue sunglasses. This habit suited the Baronne well as their bedroom antics tended to last until the dawn, and they both enjoyed Venice's vibrant nightlife, which served as a prelude before returning to the Count's palazzio on the Grand Canal. It might have been Venice's incomparable romantic atmosphere, but Carmilla found herself inextricably and inexorably failing in love with the Count, and with this came jealousy. So, she hired the segugio commonly known in Venice as "the Bloodhound."

Lorenzo Montalbano had once been the personal spy of Pope Clement XI until he had fallen foul of the powerful prelate by failing to bring to book an unchaste cardinal on the grounds that most of the other cardinals were equally or more profligate. That the fact that the aforementioned cardinal was the main candidate to be the next pope might have had something to do with both Clement's and Montalbano's motives was never in doubt. But it meant that the famous segugio was unemployed. Clement had proven far less unforgiving than his chosen name might have suggested—the Pope had made sure that Montalbano was persona non grata in

Rome, so he had removed himself to Venice. His new employer was French which meant that she was immune to Italy's intrigues not that Carmilla would have cared anyway.

Montalbano's thin, gaunt face was well suited to his profession. He looked more of a shadow than a shadow itself although, he prided himself on never casting one. But even his refined abilities were put to the limit in tracking the movements of the Count. The man seemed to be able to disappear at will. It was almost as if he knew he was being followed—which was impossible. Montalbano decided that the only way he was going to catch the Count out was by second-guessing his moves. It seemed extremely unlikely to the sleuth that the Count was carrying on an affair with another woman. He had learned of the baronne's sexual prowess, and she was undoubtedly one of the greatest beauties he had ever seen. If the Count could spend a whole night with her and then have the stamina for another female, the man must be superhuman. It therefore meant a hidden vice, overwhelmingly perverse, perhaps drugs, young boys, or a predilection for animals all of which were readily available in the back alleys of Venice. There was one strange habit of the Count that Montalbano found particularly disturbing: he often frequented the San Michele Cemetery. Did the Count have a morbid fascination with the dead, or was it something even more grotesque? He had heard of such things but had never witnessed them in person, and did not want to.

He set up camp on the Island of San Michele and waited. It was several days until the Count made an appearance. It was nearing sundown, but as usual, he was wearing his trademark blue sunglasses. He arrived in his own gondola and mingled with a small funeral cortege. Montalbano remained at a discreet distance and observed. The Count lingered by the tomb long after the other mourners had left. He seemed as still as a statue, never betraying even the slightest movement. It took all of Montalbano's considerable prowess to match him. Every limb screamed in protest as he stood his vigil. Finally, deep in the night, the Count made his move. He went to the crypt and pulled open the locked iron door as if it were plywood. Montalbano made a mental note not to engage in close physical combat with the man.

The Count entered the crypt and did not reappear. Once Montalbano decided it was safe, he crept up to the crypt. The Count had removed the corpse from her tomb and was gently cradling her. The spy was now sure he was going to be witness to a grossly indecent act. He steeled himself—it was his job, after all. But what he saw defied even his most terrible expectations. The Count had removed a small flask from his pocket and was administering its contents to the dead woman's mouth. Montalbano was sure he was witnessing a miracle—the corpse was miraculously returning to life! He had to stifle a cry, it was so—*unnatural*.

The young woman, so recently deceased, was very confused. One moment she had been at a masked ball, and the next, she was in some sort of vault. She vaguely recognized the man supporting her. She managed to ask the only the obvious question: "What happened?"

"A terrible accident, my dear, or so it would appear. You suffered an unfortunate allergic reaction to some food, or you may have been deliberately poisoned. The shock to your system sent you into a coma—a very common reaction that is often mistaken for death. I noted the symptoms but did not voice my opinions. You see, I'm a mere foreigner passing through—I would have been ridiculed. So I came here to offer a temporary remedy."

"Why temporary? Am I not restored?"

The Count sighed. "I know who you are, Angelique. I know you followed your mother here with your friends and have remained admirably incognito. I imagine it was on Kings Louis's request. Your mother is, as you no doubt know, also a great gatherer of information. Venice is in a state of flux, and where there is disunity, there is always opportunity. Some information can be very sensitive, sensitive enough to cost a life—unfortunately yours. You have not been here long enough to be privy to such secrets. The assassins must have mistaken you for your mother."

"Assassins ... So, I was murdered! But you said I was in a coma ..."

"I'm afraid I was guilty of a little disambulation. The shock is sometimes too much for those ... *reawakened* ... They need a feasible explanation, or they succumb to their real death and return to sleep the eternal sleep. I knew you would be strong enough ... I was right."

"Reawakened ... I don't understand."

The Count proceeded to explain—not only to Angelique, but also to the eavesdropping Montalbano. To most people the Count's tale would have been dismissed as plain nonsense or the ramblings of a madman. But Angelique was not most people.

"To the best of my knowledge, I am immortal. For all intents and purposes my strength appears to increase with age. When I was first 'turned,' I was just a lone vampire. A mere haemovore. A loathsome parasite that lurked in the shadows. Over the centuries I have become a Nosferatu, with more powers than you can imagine. However, that does not mean I am invulnerable and cannot be destroyed. For my own good and yours, I will not tell you how this is possible at the present moment. You have a choice now: I can leave this place and let you rest, or you can join me in the eternal night. It is not a light decision, I know, for at one time I also had to make it. You have until daylight to make your decision. I should warn you this is only the second time I have ever 'turned' another human. The first time had an unfortunate result. Now, excuse me a moment. I have another matter to attend to ... "

Montalbano watched from his hiding place as the Count did one of his disappearing acts. He swirled his cloak, and the next moment he was standing beside him. The Count gave him a pleasant smile as if he were greeting an old friend. "You know what they say about cats ... " Before Montalbano could reply, he was dead.

The Count had only been gone a moment, but in that time, Angelique had made up her mind. "Do what you must with me. I do not want death."

He drew her to him and bent her neck gently as if he were going to nuzzle it. She felt as if he were kissing her and was about to complain that this was plainly just a ruse to take advantage of her but then she had the unmistakable feeling that she was being drained of her blood. As she started to swoon, the Count tore open his shirt and ran the razor-sharp nail of his little finger just under his nipple to split open a vein. Angelique found herself suckling on it like a newborn babe—as indeed she was.

A kaleidoscope of colors and thoughts flooded into her mind. Every fresh mouthful of blood brought new ecstasies far greater than any she had ever experienced. She had glimpses of the Count's own recollections, even his many partners. Thousands of orgasms racked her body. Her body filled with light, love, and happiness. This was not the darkness she had expected; this was a dazzling rainbow of sensations. She felt more alive than she had ever felt before. The very stars were within her reach. The Count pulled her head away.

"Not too much, my love. You are young. Soon, you will experience the fever of death and rebirth. We must leave here."

With that, he wrapped her in his cloak and flew into the night sky. The fact that they were actually flying high above the City of Venice did not perturb Angelique in any way. It all seemed quite natural to her reborn self. She was a goddess in the arms of her god. It was quite natural to fly.

The Count took Angelique to one of his hideaways so he could stay with her throughout her "turning." It lasted many days, but it could have been years or seconds as far as Angelique was concerned. She inhabited a place where time had no meaning and good and evil did not exist. She was sometimes aware of the Count feeding from her and her feeding from him. She did not die ...

Baronne Carmilla Archambault never found out what really became of her daughter. She never saw Angelique or the Count again in her lifetime although, she might have been gratified to learn that they did attend her funeral—incognito, of course. She had been informed by one of King Louis XIV's agents that Angelique had been his spy and had been poisoned in Venice. But when she visited the crypt that supposedly contained the remains of her daughter, all she found was the murdered corpse of Montalbano. Everything was very discreetly hushed up and the baronne returned to France. She had lost her daughter and the only man she had ever loved. She spent the rest of her life waiting for them to return.

Once she had been reborn, Angelique was eager to explore her new powers but the Count insisted she rest. They read to each other or played cards. One night, they played a silly game of her invention. They both had to ask each other one question and they had to promise each other to answer it truthfully and never repeat it to others. The Count gave his solemn word, and she knew, in turn, that she would or could never lie to him. It fell to him to ask the first question.

He asked how her husband, the Comte, had really died. So, she told him:

On their wedding night the Comte had unsuccessfully tried to consummate their marriage, whether this failure was due to the copious amounts of alcohol he had consumed during the celebrations or just old age, she did not know or care, but it came as a great relief when he passed out whilst taking off his breeches, as the mere touch of the old man's liver-speckled hands made her skin crawl.

His failure to mount her successfully continued night after night. Her beauty so overwhelmed him that it seemingly also overpowered his penis—it would not rise to the honeyed promise between her legs. She told the Comte she would cure him of his impotence and, in all respects, would be a dutiful wife.

She started the cure the very next night. That night, and every night thereafter, she would appear in his bedchamber with one fewer garment on. She would not allow him to touch her but instead would parade before him and recline on the chaise longue or the bed in lewd and suggestive positions that would leave the Comte salivating like a dog.

After twelve days, she was down to her last garment—a flimsy silk chemise that revealed more than it covered. She swayed her hips before him provocatively and touched herself between her legs. She placed her moistened finger under the Comte's nose. He sniffed appreciatively and then sucked it voraciously. Slowly, so very slowly, that it made him tremble as he lay in his bed, she removed the last piece of clothing and stood before him completely naked. Then, deliberately taking her precious time, she languorously climbed on top of him and very delicately placed her scented and heated mound on top of the Comte's semi-erect penis, at which point, he promptly and obligingly died of a massive stroke.

The Count stifled a laugh, smiling appreciatively instead.

"My most sincere commiserations, Comtesse," he said.

Angelique's question required a more complicated and comprehensive answer. From an early age, she had immersed herself in the vast library of her father's mansion, satiating her precocious curiosity with crumbling, dusty volumes that had long been forgotten. Her father's tastes tended to veer toward the more proven natural sciences. The contents of some of the more esoteric ancient tomes imprinted themselves on her infallible memory—a trait inherited from her mother. The books told of mythical beings who lived beyond the confines of the mortal world and possessed unimaginable powers. She had always longed to meet such a being. And now she was one.

"Who made you what you are? Have vampires always existed?

"That is two questions, my sweet, but I will allow it as I know how curious you are of your new *condition*."

He started by answering her first question.

"To tell you the truth, I can't even remember who made me. It could have been a man or a woman, but given my sexual predilections, it was most

probably a woman. And it was rich, strong blood—
Nosferatu blood. It was a time before the Egyptians
had even thought of building pyramids. Whoever it
was left me to my own devices. I spent countless
years living in fear until I gradually learned how to
hide properly. As I grew older, my powers increased,
and I found I could feed less and sleep longer. I began
to learn there were others like me, but we avoided
each other—like tigers who marking their territory in
the jungle. It is the loneliness that is our undoing."

"Is that why you chose me? Angelique asked.

"No, Angelique, I think you will find it is you
who chose me. I had hoped for so long to have a
companion, but hope is a dangerous thing. And as to
your second question—I simply do not know.
Parasites have always existed, but I don't know if we
are parasites or if humans are simply there to feed us.
Perhaps we are out of kilter, a misstep in the
hopscotch game of evolution. All I know is we exist,
and that is enough for me, and it should be enough for
you. Glory in it."

The Count was surprised at how much she
knew about him. Unlike her mother, Angelique was
auto-didactic and had found out more about her
mother's new lover than any other person at court.

Angelique had tasked herself with finding out
everything she could about the mysterious Count, and
the baron had found himself sharing his beloved
library with his precocious daughter once more, but

he had politely ignored her. She found the Count's crest in a mildewed volume in one of the forgotten corners of the library. It was the exact same serpentine symbol engraved on the doors of his coach. Apparently, it had once represented the now extinct Order of the Dragon. It had belonged to a cursed prince of Wallachia who had become famous for his persecution of the Turks. It was a fanatical Christian order, and the Count did not seem in the least religiously inclined—quite the opposite, in fact. People commented he was never to be seen at mass, but these were hedonistic times, and it was not considered the great transgression it might once have been. When questioned about his origins, he was very vague. People seemed to accept the mystery as easily as they did everything else about him. Despite herself, she was attracted to him even though he was male and her mother's lover to boot—equally repugnant in their own way. She excused herself this fault because she knew that somewhere in the depths of her soul, he was more than just a man. Now she had learned the truth in the most finite way possible.

And so began their strange relationship in the darkness of the undead. Angelique proved to be a fast learner even though her first kill was sloppy. They robed themselves simple cloths and visited a nearby village, where they entered the only tavern. The Count pretended to be her ancient, doddering parent. Angelique's simple dress did nothing to disguise her voluptuous figure, and it wasn't long before all of the village's young swains were drooling at the mouth. The temporarily disregarded wenches stared at her with naked loathing. Such was the ardor that was shown to the beautiful maiden, who seemed to have been delivered from heaven itself, that violence threatened to boil over into open swordplay. The Count used fluence on the young men to calm them down and, the tension was relieved.

The Count had taught her to communicate telepathically, and he made her understand that he had singled out her prey. It was the village dunderhead, who many villagers suspected of stealing their pigs and even copulating with their sheep. She was greatly repelled by the man's aspect. He was gap-toothed, filthy, and cross-eyed to boot, but her hunger was stronger than her aversion. She found it difficult to flirt with him with any enthusiasm, not just because of his repellent looks, but also because he was not used to talking with women. He flushed and stammered over every word, making the task of seducing him practically impossible for her. The blood lust was so deep upon her, though, that it overrode any other consideration. Her determination won through in the end, and it finally dawned on the oaf that she was his for the taking. His attempts were still clumsy, but much to the confounded amazement of the young blades in the inn, he walked out accompanied by the most beautiful woman who had ever graced their village.

Angelique and the Count led him deep into the forest. The Count gradually fell behind but he encouraged them to go ahead to their non-existent caravan, saying that he wanted to take the night air. The two would-be lovers forged ahead to take their opportunity. Angelique whispered sweet words of encouragement into the ardent peasant's ear. She urged him to go ahead while she commenced disrobing. She promised him she would be free of any underclothing by the time they reached the comfort of the caravan's bed. The man practically ran. She let him gain some distance as her dainty eye teeth elongated into two-inch-long fangs and her jaw adjusted painfully to accommodate them. She fell on him from behind with a ravenous hunger, tearing his throat out in one bite and gulping down the precious liquid as it fountained out of the gaping wound. The blood tasted so good that her eyes turned in on themselves like they did when she had an orgasm.

The Count remonstrated with her for the messy kill and pointed out all the blood she had wasted. He told her that she would learn to be much less careless with her kills but that for a while, primal savagery would still get the better of her. The Count summoned wolves to dispose of the rest of the remains.

By the time they reached their underground tomb, her face had returned to something approaching normality, but it was still slightly flushed and swollen from her recent kill. Her fangs had receded inside her gums and the painful, enormous jaws had shrunk back to human size. For a moment, though, she had felt the monster she had become and what her forfeiture of humanity really meant.

They slept well the following day. The Count, who could go a long time without feeding, was content that he no longer had to feed his concubine, and Angelique was happy that she had managed her first kill by herself. It was as though the blood she carried from the Count had released an innate hunting instinct in her. It had also created an invisible bond between them. They were now united in murder—a mortal sin. And she could now see the Count's aura, a deep purple tinged with red. They could have been the colors of Hell itself she would not have minded.

They travelled throughout Europe, either on foot or flying together, with Angelique held close to the Count's chest. During their flights, the Count pointed out safe hiding places that vampires marked with a blue flame that was invisible to the mortal eye. All vampires were welcome to use these places of rest and sanctuary provided they were not occupied. Vampires never disturbed another vampire's rest except in the direst circumstance. Much of this arcane vampire lore was passed to those who had been fortunate enough to be turned by a Nosferatu. Those vampires who had been turned by ordinary or young vampires were not so lucky and many perished before gaining such knowledge.

They never lingered long in one area and avoided any of their kind by a natural instinct. The Count had never consciously met another vampire, least of all a Nosferatu (except, perhaps the once). He could not even remember who had 'turned' him, yet he could sense their presence from far away. Vampires tended to avoid each other simply because it would be unwise to share the same hunting ground. It would never do for mortals to even suspect of their existence.

The Count warned her that there were some amongst the mortals who knew the ancient legends to be true, and these 'vampire hunters' were more ruthless and sadistic than most of the vampires they hunted. They killed purely for pleasure or to satisfy some innate desire. They often used religion as an excuse for their barbarity. It was because of these hunters that it was never desirable to attract unwanted attention to oneself. However, he assured Angelique, the hunters gave away their presence by the smell of unholy death they carried with them, so she would have ample warning that they were in her vicinity. Like all her senses, her sense of smell was now many times that of a human, along with her now abnormal and superhuman strength. He could not describe the stink they carried to her, but he assured her that she would recognize it once she had smelled it.

They journeyed across the sea to England, where they met a gorgeous young English rose called Dorotea Fanshaw, with whom they both immediately fell in love. The love was mutual. Dorotea already possessed the abnormal gift of second sight and a crude form of telepathy. She sensed who and what they were, and she made it known to them that she wished to join them. She was tired of the stiff conventions of the English upper class. Angelique and Dorotea both begged him the Count to 'turn' her. He found it difficult to refuse, such beautiful women, so the duo, before long, became a trio.

They left England for Paris where 'The Terror', was just beginning. The thirsty guillotine could be heard doing its terrible work all over Paris, the streets ran with blood, and the city smelt like an abattoir. The smell was overpowering for the vampires, and for once, they found themselves amongst other vampires, who, attracted by the bloodbath, were glutting themselves.

The Count and his two concubines made a point of only slaughtering the worst of the fanatical mob, singling out murderers and sadists. It was in Paris that they met two recently turned female vampires, a German and a French woman who had been lovers in real life and had been turned by a sadistic aristocrat vampire without their consent.

They, in turn, had betrayed him to the mob, who had beheaded him in his coffin, and then dragged his corpse into the raging sunlight of midday, where it spontaneously combusted. They were spurned by other vampires for the great sin they had committed. It was an unwritten law that no vampire should betray another vampire.

The trio knew they had found kindred spirits in the two outlawed vampires despite the crime they had committed against their own kind. After all, they themselves were not the usual cadre of vampires. The three became five. The Count was very contented that he now possessed his own personal harem and he was just as pleased with participating in their mutual sexual pleasures as he was observing them satisfying each other.

When The Terror imploded and reached its inevitable and bloody conclusion they voyaged to the New World, where they recruited a Southern belle named Miss April Lovelace into their unholy group and a sultry Trinidadian from the bayous of New Orleans who went by the name Selene Felonise. The Count then decided enough was enough. The seven of them made a perfect and inseparable group.

They opened a brothel in Baton Rouge, which became their perfect cover, and there lived happily. They employed only the most beautiful prostitutes to fulfill their regular clients' needs while they personally took care of solitary visitors who would not be missed.

During the American Civil War they once again feasted well. Amidst the chaos and carnage, their kind of bloodletting went unnoticed. They decided to return to Europe during the political and financial ruin in the aftermath of the Union's victory. The Count and his concubines had found that the bitter aftertaste of a country that had split itself in twain was not to their liking.

In the refuge of the Count's castle, he taught them the blessings of the Long Sleep after which they would find themselves refreshed and stronger but, of course, famished beyond imagination, a trait that the Count was at pains to restrain. One ravenous vampire was dangerous enough but six suddenly let loose on the world was highly likely to attract unwanted attention.

They had been awoken by the human monster Heydrich, and it had resulted in his inevitable demise. The vampires slept again, but they were about to experience an unexpected reawakening.

CHAPTER EIGHT

STALINGRAD

The belief in the possibility of a short decisive war appears to be one of the most ancient and dangerous of human illusions

Robert Wilson Lynd

The funeral service for Heydrich was by far the most momentous in its pomp and majesty in the history of the Third Reich, even surpassing that of Horst Wessel, whose song they played. Himmler had attended quite a few, but this was the most boringly ceremonious. In an odd way, he felt kind of jealous. He idly wondered if he should be preparing the arrangements for his own funeral. He could not leave it in the hands of others—they would not be able to do justice to the more magnificent ceremony he had in mind. It would put Heydrich's in the shade.

When it came time for the Reichsführer of the Schutzstaffel turn to pay his respects, Himmler leaned over the prone body of his former protégé and pretending to kiss Heydrich's forehead, he whispered in the corpse's ear instead.

"I know you can hear me, Heydrich. I guessed what the vampires did to you. It must be terrible in there for you. You will be glad to learn I will put our friends to better use than you have done and will earn the enduring love of the Führer and the Fatherland, while you will just become a lost footnote in history."

He stepped away with a barely concealed smile, which he hid with his sleeve, pretending to wipe away a tear.

The Führer was less restrained and had to be supported away from the coffin. He had never made a secret of the fact that Heydrich was one of his favorites.

The Count was not pleased to be woken once again. It seemed to him as if he had only just closed his eyes. He restrained himself from slaughtering the soldiers there and then. It was now apparent to him that these loathsome creatures known as Nazis were not going to disappear out of his world quite as easily as he had expected. Despite their great powers, his 'girls' were still relatively young, and, as such, vulnerable. The Count knew he would not be able to protect them from the full might of the Nazis. He also suspected that he had somehow been played by

Himmler. The Reichsführer, he suspected, had something up his sleeve. It was something terrible, and the Count wanted to know what it was. So it was that the vampires found themselves once again immersed in the Nazis' plans for world domination.

Far away from Berlin, an SS lieutenant was in a freezing foxhole outside Stalingrad, listening to the regular 9:55 PM broadcast from Radio Belgrade of "Lily Marleen". He was stoutly resisting the urge to scratch at his lice infested chest. He knew that doing so would only make it worse. He also knew that his men were worse off than him. At least he could vaguely remember having had a bath and what it felt like. He was, nevertheless, proud of his half-starved, lice-infested, stinking soldiers who shared the hole he had spent the last few days in. They were on minimum rations and cut off from their comrades, but not one of them had muttered a word of complaint. None of them knew what they were doing there or what or whom they were waiting for. He wondered if they would have been shocked to learn that he did not know much more than them, or if they would have really cared. Most of the German soldiers he knew in Stalingrad did not care much about anything except staying alive. Maybe he had underestimated his soldiers, and they were just glad to be behind the lines and out of range of the deadly Russian snipers. A mangy dog appeared from nowhere, a green, gangrenous hand clamped between its jaws. It had no doubt been scavenging around one of the field hospitals, where there were easy pickings of discarded human meat. The soldiers chased it away with some well-aimed stones.

The "Lily Marleen" was meant to be the signal for the arrival of some special boxes, which they were to guard with their lives. He had been told, or rather ordered, not to move until they had arrived, and then they would be given further instruction. But the boxes had still not arrived after several days, and it looked like it would be another no-show tonight. On top of that, it seemed to be even more freezing than usual, if that were possible. It looked like they could be in for a blizzard.

Then, out of the impending snowstorm, an incongruous sight met their eyes: a black wagon with horses in equally black plumage pulling a cart carrying wooden coffins. There hadn't been animals on the Eastern Front for a long time—they had all been eaten a long, long time ago.

The wagon was driven by wild-eyed gypsies who whipped the steeds cruelly and without mercy. They pulled to a jolting halt just in front of the soldier's foxhole as if they could sense it. As soon as they had finished unloading the cart with the soldiers' help they took off into the snowstorm as if they had never been there in the first place. Not a word was exchanged.

The soldiers looked longingly at the horses' rapidly disappearing hoof prints as if they could magically transmogrify the animals receding presence into huge, juicy steaks.

Then they turned their attention to the battered wooden coffins. They appeared to be unremarkable apart for some strange rune-like characters inscribed on their lids. The men dragged them into the foxhole and awaited the promised orders. They didn't have to wait for too long. The night was suddenly split by the most sustained bombing they had ever seen. Above Stalingrad hung a strange vision: the huge black cloud produced by the bombing had the ghastly shape of a huge black cross.

Then the coffins opened by themselves ...

The soldiers watched in horror as the beautiful female vampires levitated from the coffins. They had been ordered to guard the boxes with their lives but they had not expected this. Was it a new kind of secret weapon? They had heard rumors of strange experiments being carried out in Poland. The lieutenant mistakenly ordered his men to stand down—the beautiful women had a bewitching effect on him. It did not last long as the vampires fell upon the men. They wasted no time in seduction and speedily dispatched them all within seconds.

The Count looked around the battlefield in disgust. He now deeply regretted the pact he had made with Himmler, who had promised the Count the luxury all of Moscow in return for their collaboration in the taking of Stalingrad. The offer had proved too tempting. Now, as he surveyed the devastation ahead of him, he realized it might have been a huge mistake.

They made their way like shadows into the ruins of what had once been a great city—the Count remembered its heyday. The city stank of corpses, but there were plenty of live humans for them to feed on and many places where they could take their day sleep. But it was squalid and did not suit any of the vampires—it was not what they were accustomed to. They fed mostly on children and sickly survivors who were condemned an icy death anyway. Gradually, it became difficult to differentiate between the Russians and the Germans—everyone was just a survivor, and they survived by behaving more like animals than human beings. In fact, the animals, those left alive, were genteel compared to their mammalian counterparts.

The Count had carried out Himmler's wishes, but as far as he could see, the terror and mayhem they were meant to produce was already there. Moscow's supposed luxuries seemed a long way off. His girls satisfied themselves in hot orgies, but the blood they drained was weak, sour, and full of fear. Angelique had mentioned to the Count, whilst chewing on a pair of Russian soldier's testicles that despite the German soldiers' best efforts to thwart the weather, it would take a terrible toll on the Wehrmacht. The Count was inclined to agree. It was also impossible to break through frozen flesh to find warm blood—the vampires would suffer as much as both armies, but not as much as the civilians, who were the real casualties of Stalingrad.

When the vampires did come upon a Russian soldier, they did not just drain him but ripped him apart to spread fear as per Himmler's instructions. There was no terror in Stalingrad—as though the people and soldiers had seemingly become immune to it. The horror of the city was worse than even vampires could produce.

The Count who could read minds very well had learned that there were experiments taking place in Poland that interested him very much. As for Hitler's plans to take Stalingrad the Count considered them ridiculous. He had sacrificed the whole of the 6th Army, and as far as the Count was concerned, it was the beginning of the end. But before he left he wanted to give his girls a treat. They had discovered a relatively safe cellar for themselves where they could sleep during sunlight hours. He had a very large, round bathtub, that he had acquired from one of the ancient mansions. He hung somnambulant soldiers above a large copper funnel, which connected to the tub, by hooks through their ankles. He slit their throats with his razor-sharp talons. They did not stir from the pleasant dreams the Count had blessed them with. Their warm blood gradually filled the tub in which his girls could bathe and drink at their will.

Back in Berlin, Hitler was throwing one of his tantrums. He was taking it out on Himmler.

"You told me we would have Stalingrad months ago. Instead we have traitorous bastards who are asking that they be allowed to surrender."

Hitler thumped his fist on the desk. "There will be no surrender. They will fight to the last man. And in the future any General that suggests withdrawal or surrender will be shot immediately."

Himmler decided it would be best not to remind Hitler that it had been Hitler's that it had been his decision to split the 6th Army in two against all military tactical common sense and also against all of his generals' advice.

"And what of your so-called vampires. They were supposed to be the game-changers. They have done nothing as far as I can see."

Hitler stormed around the room scattering documents everywhere.

"We still have The Bell project in Poland and the Antarctica project," Himmler said.

"Fuck The Bell and Antarctica projects ... I want results now!" Hitler screeched.

Himmler saluted and made a quick exit.

Stalingrad was eerily quiet. There was the occasional mortar fire and rifle shots from snipers, but the usual bombardments had ceased. There was a sense in the city that something was about to happen and the Count sensed it would not be good for the Wehrmacht. The soldiers had long ago given up any idea of taking the city. Most of them were starving or freezing to death, but they still fought on even though there was no hope for them. Surrender was really the only option, but then, the Russians were hardly lenient with prisoners of war, and their conditions would hardly change. They faced death from all quarters.

The Count had a secret admiration for both armies. He had always considered humans weak, but Stalingrad was a revelation. In his cold heart, he felt some twinkling of admiration and sympathy for both sides, and he did not like having feelings for mortals. He had learned of secret experiments being carried out in a fortified bunker in Poland with something called "The Bell", a levitation device that he considered would be of great use to him. His girls, apart from Angelique, were not strong enough to fly the distances between vampires' safe vaults, and a sojourn in Poland would be the perfect solution.

The girls cavorted in the blood-filled bathtub, and the Count joined in. Bathing in blood was one of the girls' chief delights and the Count had made sure the funnel was plentifully supplied. They drank and licked each other until they had had their fill. Then the Count told them of his plan and as he had expected they were all enthusiastic. They exited the tub, and the blood they were covered in was instantly absorbed into their skins making them more beautiful and youthful than ever.

The time had come for them to move and for the Count to acquire The Bell.

CHAPTER NINE

THE BELL

If opportunity doesn't knock, build a door.

Milton Berle

Himmler was as devastated as Hitler at the loss at Stalingrad. He could see the beginning of the end on the horizon. It made him shudder—he recalled Churchill's prophetic speech after the victory at El Alamein, "Now this is not the end. It is not even the beginning of the end. But it is, perhaps, the end of the beginning."

That was just over a year ago, but with the destruction of the 6th Army at Stalingrad, all the strategic initiative on the Eastern Front had been lost, and with it, quite possibly, the war. He might have to contemplate the unthinkable—a deal with the Allies. His secret agents had informed him that "Der Dicke" Göring was contemplating much the same thing. He would have to play his cards close to his vest and gather in his bargaining chips.

He returned to the sanctuary of Wewelsburg Castle, away from the manic, drug-fueled wrath of the Führer, where he performed various Kundalini yoga asanas to relax himself. The Count and his cadre of female vampires had gone AWOL. They had failed in their duty to the Third Reich and the Führer, but more importantly, they had reneged on their deal with him. The vampires had not delivered Stalingrad to the Wehrmacht, and neither Hitler or Himmler were known for being forgiving. He summoned members of the Thule and Vril Societies for a ritual to visualize the vampires and pinpoint their location. They gathered along with other elite SS in the basement of the castle around the engraving on the marble floor known as the Black Sun. All they could manage to come up with was an image of a giant black bell.

Himmler winced at the abstruse mention of Die Glocke. It was meant to be top secret. Private consultations with the Vril Society's mysterious medium, the Lady in Black, Maria Orsik, supposedly a direct link to the Aryan aliens on planet Aldebaran, confirmed it. It was enough to convince Himmler that somehow, the Count had learned of The Bell's/Die Glocke's existence. Maria Orsik had even gone so far as to warn Himmler that a great ripple in the fabric of time stretching backwards was disturbing the aether, and the Black Sun itself was in danger.

A troubled Himmler stared down at the design on the floor of the North Tower of Wewelsburg Castle: the dark, chromatic sun wheel mosaic located in the center of the hall—the Black Sun (Schwarze Sonne abbreviated to SS). What did all these revelations mean? Was the castle itself in danger or the secret Orders of the Thule and the Vril-Gesellschaft along with his treasured SS? It all boiled down to what the Count was up to. There was no doubt in Himmler's mind that the vampires were the prophesied peril. He sent for the most secret of his secret agents. His ace in the hole—Abraham Van Helsing.

The Count was hanging upside down in his bat form, observing his frolicking brood. The bewitching but fatal femme vampires were bathing in tubs of blood, freshly supplied by a recently slaughtered platoon of German soldiers. Like them, the soldiers had been escaping from the hell that was Stalingrad, and unfortunately for them, they had run into the hell that was the vampires. He wanted his girls well fed and rested. They had a long, cold journey ahead. The Count had learned in the killing fields of Stalingrad about the Wunderwaffe or Wonder Weapon, being developed by the Germans at a secret location on the Czechoslovakian border near Poland—The Bell, due to its bizarre shape. For some time, his rest had been disturbed by strange vibrations running through the netherworld he inhabited—finally. he had the explanation. The Germans, it seemed, were experimenting with something they did not fully understand or could control. The Count was sure of this the vibrations were wrong. It was as if someone were pounding their fists futilely on the wrong door. Unfortunately, they were waking up the wrong people ... or things.

  The Count had unsuccessfully interrogated by mind control nearly every Nazi officer he sensed knew something of Die Glocke. But they either knew very little or the same rumors the Count had already heard. He would feed the officers to the grateful girls after he had finished with them. They were generally in slightly better condition than the common soldiers, but not by much. Practically everyone on the Russian front was on the verge of starvation, and their blood was always poor fare. But there were always other delights to make up for it. He changed into his human form and joined the girls.

Abraham Van Helsing was accustomed to being given bizarre orders by the Reichsführer of the Schutzstaffel, but tracking down a vampire was one of the more unusual. He was, of course, as a member of the elite Thule Society, quite familiar with the occult and Himmler's ardent interest in it. He knew enough about vampires to know that it was better to disregard most of the fictional accounts about them—

they were fairy stories meant to scare children. A crucifix, for example, would not affect a vampire except to perhaps make it more scornful of the human bandying it—holy objects, he had been given to understand, only had an effect on a vampire if the vampire itself believed in them. He had learned there was an important difference between the pre-Christian Nosferatu and the post-Christian vampires. This difference extended to the weapons you could use against them or to protect yourself from them. Some were so ancient that they had been old when Jesus had been nailed to the cross. And some had even been worshipped as gods by pagan followers even before the pyramids had been raised on desert sands, even when then Sphinx had been young.

The question that most intrigued Van Helsing, though, was how did one spy on a vampire? A being that if it did exist, would no doubt have supernatural powers, that would render it impervious to Van Helsing's normal methods of espionage.

The information that Himmler had given him on the vampires was very vague, which made Van Helsing worried. Himmler was usually meticulous, so it meant he was holding something back on purpose. The Reichsführer, quite rightly, in Van Helsing's opinion, only ever told you as much as you needed to know, but on this occasion, he had excelled himself and left Van Helsing completely in the dark as to the purpose or true nature of the mission. Van Helsing had been told airily that he was to locate the cadre of vampires without them knowing, confirm it, and report back. It was almost as if Himmler were so wary of these so-called vampires he did not want them to know that he was interested in their actions. Information gathering was Van Helsing's forte. The Reichsführer obviously thought that Helsing would dig up the information that he required as he went along. And that was literally what Van Helsing was doing at that very moment—digging.

So far, he had disinterred several corpses that had, supposedly, been drained of their blood by vampires. The vampires, now long gone, were remembered by those lucky enough to avoid their attentions. The descriptions, however vague, fit those of the Count and his femme fatales. Of the many corpses surrounding Stalingrad attributed to the vampires, he noticed that the majority were NKVD officers—hated by the German and Russian soldiers alike. All of the faces of the dead men spoke of an indelible terror, as though they had been witness to some horror that went far beyond the narrow confines of human understanding. The only time Van Helsing had seen such expressions, it had been under the most severe physical and psychological torture. They must have been privy to an awful vision beyond the reaches of mortal imagination. He knew instinctively that he must get hold of a soldier who had survived the ungodly ordeal, if there was one. He had to find out why the vampires had tortured these particular individuals. As far as he was he was aware, the vampires did not usually bother with such crude methods. To them the humans were mere cattle carrying the fluid that was essential to their survival, and they treated them accordingly.

As luck would have it, he heard of a high-ranking SS officer who had been relieved of his duties after blabbering on about vampires and the forces of darkness. He had been confined to some sort of lunatic asylum on the outskirts of Poland. It was as though he had been hidden away by the Nazis because they were ashamed of him. The officer had been decorated with the Iron Cross and other medals of valor—a man not easily frightened, you would guess, and one that the German high command could not safely execute and brush under the carpet. Combat fatigue was a label that hid many sins, and it was a convenient reason for semi-incarceration.

Van Helsing found the asylum a disused chateau that seemed to house just the lunatic colonel, a doctor, and a nurse. He showed the doctor the Reichsführer's pass, which opened all doors. The doctor was reluctant to disturb his patient, who was under heavy sedation but the warning flash in Van Helsing's eyes made him realize that this was not a man you refused lightly.

The SS-Oberführer was sitting quietly in a wheelchair in a pleasantly sunlit room. He was looking out of a tall window. His face was expressionless, but the crimson, bloodshot eyes were not they were alert like those of a trapped fox. He took Van Helsing in with one swift glance from head to toe.

"Did Himmler send you?" he asked.

"In a way, but he did not send me directly, no," Van Helsing said.

"I know why you have come. You know, that neither God, nor Himmler, will protect you if you go looking for them."

"I protect myself."

"Then you are either very brave or a fool. Go and hide in Switzerland or somewhere until this blows over. If I could, I would come with you,"— the colonel shrugged— "for all the good it would do me." His eyes flitted this way and that. "They could come for me at any time so I must remain still as a rock."

Although his eyes darted everywhere he did not move a muscle. For the first time, he showed signs of the insanity of which he was the true prisoner.

"Do you have premonitions?" he asked Van Helsing.

"Not that I am aware, but I believe it is common amongst the soldiery."

"When death is all around you, you can sense it. Death becomes your faithful shadow. The Count you seek comes from the shadows. You will meet him. I see it in your eyes. He is waiting for you."

Despite himself, Van Helsing felt a chill leak down his spine. The colonel's piercing eyes looked deep into him as if he were searching his soul. He suddenly grabbed Van Helsing by the arm and pulled him close. It was the only movement he'd made the whole time Van Helsing had been interviewing him.

"You will find him in a place called Der Riese, near a mine called Wenceslaus, close to the Czech border," the colonel whispered. He looked around furtively, as if someone would overhear, although they were completely alone.

Van Helsing stood patted the invalid on the shoulder, and took his leave. Then he drove off at breakneck speed, ordering his chauffer to make for Czechoslovakia as fast as possible. He left so quickly he did not have time to hear the nurse's cry for the doctor. She had just discovered the lifeless body of the colonel, still seated facing the window, his hollow face set in a terrible rictus, his mouth open in a soundless scream of infinite dread. The doctor could find no pulse because there was no blood to make it. Rigor mortis was already setting in on the extravasated corpse.

Professor Walther Gerlach carefully poured the violet metallic liquid code-named, Xerum 525, from the lead-encased thermos into the two counter-rotating cylinders. His assistants stood at a respectful distance, although it was not so much out of respect for their leader, but out of a well-justified fear of the device he was pouring the Xerum 525 into. Several scientists had already died during Gerlach's experiments. The huge black bell-shaped device stood motionless at the moment, but it would start to rotate very soon, and with it, the laws of universal physics would change in ways that once harnessed could provide the key to existence.

The Count felt the aether stir. He was getting nearer to the mine and the effects of the Nazi's new weapon were more keenly felt. Angelique even mentioned feeling it, and she was a relative newborn. The scientists obviously did not know what they were dealing with. The device was out of control, but nevertheless, they might gain a glimpse of the workings of the universe, which might prove too much for their scientifically straitjacketed minds. It was time he relieved them of the object—it would not be good for them.

As Van Helsing got nearer to his objective, it became easier to follow the vampires' path. They had left a trail of drained corpses that a blind man could follow. He couldn't help, but think that it was hardly up to his detective skills. It was almost as if the Count were leaving a trail of breadcrumbs for him to follow, but this was no fairy tale and it was unlikely to have a happy ending.

Die Glocke started its rotation. The scientists ran madly down the tunnel for the welcome cover of the reinforced concrete bunker at its end. The bunker meant safety. It meant life. Gerlach was in the lead. It always came as a great surprise to the other scientists how fast the elderly, pear-shaped professor could run. There were always the laggards, of course. These were nearly always newcomers who had not yet seen The Bell in action.

A sound like a swarm of angry wasps followed them down the tunnel—The Bell was gathering momentum. Most of them made it to the bunker in time, but two of the newcomers had evidently not realized the gravity of the situation— literally. The two scientists were being pulled back toward the laboratory and the lurking, sinister hulk of Die Glocke and its gravitational field. The last scientists through the bunker's door saw that it was all up with the their lagging comrades. The other scientists slammed the steel door shut and bolted it. The bunker was windowless, but inside, there were electric lighting and monitoring equipment. It was also impervious to the screams from the scientists left outside as their blood started to gel and separate into crystals under their skin. Then they simply melted. All that was remained of them was a greasy, simmering pool on the floor. Sometime later, when The Bell had ceased spinning and had cooled somewhat, the scientists cautiously emerged.

The Count left his girls in the woods on the outskirts of the abandoned mine. Der Riese was an apt name for the secret underground complex—it was huge. Der Riese was designed as a complex labyrinth, and gaining unauthorized access was considered virtually impossible. At the heart of the labyrinth was the laboratory, and the only way to reach that was by traversing an underground canal in a dingy. It had once been a tunnel before it had been flooded with acrid black waters. The canal was booby-trapped along its entire length. Even touching its sides meant instant death. At the end of the canal was a reinforced bunker that housed a powerful machine gun. The gun's stocky barrel protruded from a slit and was trained directly on the water. It was manned twenty-four hours a day. Any guard who was not at complete attention inside Der Riese was shot on the spot. It would be extremely difficult for any mortal man to get through to that laboratory, but the Count was not any mortal man.

The guards paid no attention to the bat. There were always lots of them flitting in and out the tunnels. They did not notice anything unusual about its behavior apart from the fact that it chose to hang upside directly above Die Glocke, an unfortunate place to rest, they decided. It would not be long until the bat would end up as just another splash of grease gracing The Bell's sides. They made some halfhearted bets amongst themselves on the length of its mortality.

Gerlach stepped over the puddled remains of what had once been two of the leading young German physicists of their day. He tutted. It really was a shame, but they had died in the name of science—what could be nobler? Now he had more important matters to attend to. The mixture still needed a lot more refining, but he was sure he was making progress. At least the deaths were getting fewer or maybe his assistants were getting fitter. One day soon, they would try a manned flight, needless to say, with one of his assistants at the controls.

The Count had no real need to observe what the scientist was doing—he could sense it. The idiot was still meddling in powers far beyond the scope of his technical ability. It was also beyond the scope of the Count's, although he knew that if he devoted several lifetimes to the problem of the elixir that ran the machine he would discover its true potential. But what use had an immortal being for a time machine? For that was what The Bell was—its ultimate reality. But as usual, the Nazis only saw one side of its purpose, that of a war machine. A temporal displacement machine was indeed capable of being a weapon of mass destruction there was no doubt about that. Time was the most destructive force in the universe.

The gravitational pull from Die Glocke made it difficult for the Count to read Gerlach's mind. He wanted to know how much Gerlach had guessed of The Bell's true potential. He had an idea that the professor had guessed some part of it but was not revealing it to the other scientists.

Van Helsing looked at the entrance of the underground bunker through his camouflaged Leitz binoculars. From the outside, it appeared deserted, but he had already paid a cursory visit to the nearby SS battalion's quarters. It housed at least a hundred men. The place, whatever it was, was very well guarded. He had already made up his mind that the Count was probably already inside the secret bunker. Now he was presented with two choices: he could show his orders to whoever was in charge of the place and play into the Count's hand, who seemed to be expecting him, or he could wait to see if the vampires revealed themselves. He was certain that the Count had brought him here deliberately, and he wanted to know why. His choice, in the end, was neither of the two. He would take the initiative—he would hunt the vampires. Van Helsing, *the Vampire Hunter.* He smiled. He liked the sound of that.

Angelique was hungry, but the Count had been very specific that they should not take any of the guards, and in particular the strange man dressed in leather hunting clothes who was clumsily spying on the Germans. As well as his bizarre choice in clothes, he had an equally idiosyncratic (some would say eccentric) choice in weapons. He carried an enormous handgun in an equally huge leather holster. It was a Gabbett-Fairfax Mars pistol, which had a fearsome reputation as one of the most powerful handguns in the world. It had been rejected by the English military because it 'kicked' a lot. One general had been known to have remarked, 'No man who fired this would wish to fire it a second time'. It would have no problem stopping a vampire as it would no doubt blow anything within its vicinity into very small pieces. There were said to be only a few in existence. They were highly coveted for the terrible damage they could inflict on an enemy, and sometimes on the wielder himself. It was not just ill-famed for its tremendous recoil, but the noise it made had resulted in several owners having long-term hearing problems. This was generally overlooked at the time due to most of the owners' fragile mental states after discharging the pistol and the pandemonium that ensued.

The man was supposed to be some kind of secret agent. If that was what he was, then he wasn't was a very good one, she decided. Her acute senses knew where he was at any given moment. And at that moment, he appeared to be studying some sort of plant. He was rubbing the leaves between his fingers and then sniffing them. He had been doing this for some time, just wandering aimlessly in circles, carelessly discarding the leaves of the plant as he went on his ambling way.

It had been easier to trap a vampire than Van Helsing had imagined. He had found the entrapment spell long ago in a sixteenth-century grimoire. He had not placed much stock in it—he never did with things connected with magick—but it seemed to be working just fine. The instructions had been quite clear. In order for the spell to work, it had to be fresh garlic, picked by moonlight, and it had to be laid in a wide circle around the vampire with no more than a meter separating the broken leaves and stems. The vampire, he knew from the scant information that Himmler had supplied him with, was none other than the Count's own second-in-command, a female named Angelique. The vampiress was so full of self-confidence and arrogance that it would never occur to her that the person she was spying on was actually letting her do it while laying a trap at the same time.

Angelique got bored with watching the human tottering around immersed in his weird botanical fetish. Dawn was fast approaching, and it would soon be time for her to rest—her little death, as she liked to call it. She started to glide back to the disused mineshaft the vampires had made their temporary sanctuary. Suddenly, it was as if she had hit an invisible wall. She pushed hard at the air in front of her but it would not budge. It was as if she were looking into the woods through a very clear but impassable window.

The stranger appeared before her. It was as if he were in a bubble. Not only had he ensnared her, but he was using something else to protect himself. She felt a mounting sense of alarm. This was no ordinary mortal foe. The Count had been right to warn her of him. With all her strength, she sent a telepathic message for help to the Count. The man approached her. He put his face close to hers, just outside the invisible barrier that now surrounded her. He tilted his head slightly as if he were studying a strange phenomenon that could do him no harm, like a curiously colored beetle.

"Sorry if I have temporarily discombobulated you but it will soon be daylight. You will need some shade. I know that sunlight is harmful to your kind. If you tell me what I need to know I will let you go and rejoin your happy brood."

Angelique controlled her emotions well and did not let the shock she felt at her entrapment show on her face. How did he know about her and the others? And who the hell talked like that! More importantly, she was no day-walker like the ancient. She was in real danger from sunlight. The Count had taught her how to survive for some hours after dawn, but how long could she last under the full glare of daylight? She did not want to test it—just a moment of sunlight was sheer agony. She decided to call his bluff. She deliberately sat down in as relaxed a manner as she could manage under the circumstances.

"You have made a grievous error," she said, studying her nails nonchalantly. "It will end up costing you your life."

"Really?" He sounded genuinely interested. He sat down opposite her, making himself comfortable against the trunk of a nearby tree. "I think not." He took out a cheroot, lit it, and breathed out a perfect ring of smoke.

Angelique waved her hands in disgust, "Do you mind not smoking? Some men have the vilest manners."

"I can't say that ripping someone's throat out and drinking them dry of their blood counts as very genteel behavior, my dear woman. Although, I must say, I do enjoy a rare steak now and again. And of course there are many other pleasures to be had from flesh other than killing it."

He eyed Angelique speculatively, "I expect you could give a man a great deal of pleasure if you put your mind to it."

"You really are a vile specimen of a man. Indeed, I can scarcely class you in the same species as even an animal. It would do them a great disservice."

Van Helsing glanced up at the sky. It was starting to lighten. "Ah, the dawn. One of the best times of the day, so they tell me. I rarely get a chance to see it."

"No doubt, if you took the trouble of opening one of the many whores' windows whom you no doubt spend your nights with, you might enjoy them more often. Or perhaps it is a man's bed you prefer. There is an effeminate air about you. I can only reason that you must be a sexual pervert to go around dressed in leather shorts such as yours."

"Tut, tut. And here you are, dressed in an SS major's uniform, an abhorrent costume if ever there was one. I was surprised Hugo Boss let himself be talked into designing it."

"You will pay dearly when my soldiers come for me," Angelique said. She was trying hard not to cry with terror.

"Your soldiers? I'm not aware that a deserter can command any soldiers. And while we are on the topic, Reichsführer Himmler really would appreciate a little chat with you and your master, the Count."

"I don't know what you are talking about," she said through gritted teeth as the first thin rays of the dawn's sun burned through her skin.

"Come now, Angelique. I really do not enjoy torturing people. I leave that sort of thing to your friends in the Gestapo. Evidently, they have some sick people who revel in that kind of thing." He reached into his rucksack and produced a parasol. He went to hand it to her.

"I was mistaken Herr ...? You are a gentleman, after all. I have delicate skin and do not allow it to be blemished by the sun," she said, trying her utmost to keep up the pretense. She gave him the most beguiling smile she could manage under the circumstances.

"Oh, please! This is getting tiresome." He tossed her the parasol. "Let us at least drop this charade. My name is Abraham Van Helsing, at your service. I already know who and what you are, Angelique Agoult d"Archambault."

She opened the parasol and could not help letting out a gasp of exquisite pleasure as the welcome coolness seeped right through to her bones.

"Well, sir," she said, with more equanimity now, "it looks as if you have the better of me. But have no doubt, the Count will be here soon and I can tell you whatever arcane powers you possess will be no match for his."

"I have no qualms about that, for I have no quarrel with the Count, nor, indeed, with any of you. I am what you might call a secret agent, but I serve no master save myself. And I have the good sense to know when to back the winning side. I'm afraid our jackbooted friends are about to get their comeuppance. You might do better ridding yourself of that uniform you are wearing altogether. The Allies take a dim view of the SS. And I am sure you would look quite ravishing without it."

Angelique could not help but give a coquettish smile. Even she enjoyed the occasional flattery. "Maybe another time." She flashed him a pearly white smile.

Van Helsing continued with his inquiry. "The Führer has become a drug-addled maniac, and Himmler is already making deals with the Allies behind his back. I'm not sure about Bormann though." Van Helsing seemed to have wandered off into his own thoughts. He recovered himself. He looked deep into Angelique's eyes, "What's it like being immortal?"

"No one is immortal," Angelique said.

"That you know of ... "

"That I know of." She nodded.

"I wish the Count would hurry up. These cheroots won't smoke themselves," Van Helsing said, taking another one of the long, slim cigars from the pocket of his lederhosen.

"Don't mind if I do," the Count said, taking it lightly from his fingers.

Van Helsing gazed up at the cloaked figure before him. The Count was a man for whom suave and louche were mere understatements. His face was handsome, thin and quite exceedingly cruel. His hair was so blonde, he could pass for an albino, and his tight, classic suit told you exactly what expensive tailoring looked like. It was a shade of white that dared you to stain it, and its only adornment was a bright crimson cravat and handkerchief. He was nonchalantly at ease, even in the sunlight.

"Really, Count! You mustn't go around startling people like that. You'll be the death of them," Van Helsing said. He lit another cigar for himself and then the Count's.

"What a delightful spot you've picked," the Count said, settling himself down opposite Van Helsing. "We should have brought a picnic."

"With me as the main course, no doubt," Van Helsing smiled.

Angelique, coughed discreetly. Somewhere along the line, her presence seemed to have been forgotten.

The Count smiled benevolently at her. "Off you go, my pretty," he said, blowing out an appreciative plume of smoke.

The invisible cage in which she had been held had disappeared, she realized happily. She scampered off, eager to regain the musky, coolness of the mine. The cold darkness would be bliss. She did not give Van Helsing a second thought—the Count would take care of him.

The Count picked up some nearby leaves and rubbed them between his fingers. He gave them a sniff. "Wild garlic," he commented. "I haven't heard of this spell being performed since the middle ages. You must be quite a scholar, sir."

"No scholar, but I know where to look for the information I want," Van Helsing's eyes twinkled.

"I too know where to look," the Count replied.

Van Helsing felt the Count trying to probe his mind. He had expected as much, and knew how to combat it. The Count was very strong, but he, in turn, sensed that Helsing was no fool. Van Helsing would give up his life rather than the information he possessed—he knew it was his only bargaining tool. The Count could feel that. Both of them knew that Van Helsing's life depended on the information contained within his mind—without it, he was worthless. There was no room for exchange. Torture would serve no purpose—Van Helsing had set trapdoors in his mind that would shut it down if they were breached. Besides, the Count wanted Van Helsing alive and on his side.

"Why don't we just talk," Van Helsing suggested diplomatically.

"A commendable proposal," the Count said. "What exactly does Himmler want now?"

"What every megalomaniac ever wants— complete world domination."

"So boring and yet so predictable. I'm afraid he may have missed that particular train." The Count flicked his head in the general direction of the bunker. "Does he realize the full power of the device?"

"No. If he did, we wouldn't be having this conversation," Van Helsing said. His interests did not only include the occult, but also stretched to metaphysics. He had some inkling of The Bell's true potential.

"Why haven't you attempted to steal it for yourself?" the Count asked. "I'm sure a man of your diverse skills could manage it."

Van Helsing flicked his ash. "It seems to me that the human race is intent on destroying itself as it is. I have no wish to contribute to it. That thing in there opens up a whole new Pandora's box. I have a feeling the device has already been used in its true form, and the fact that we are talking about it means a temporal paradox has either been circumvented or is about to be triggered."

The Count nodded—he was impressed with Van Helsing. "And how do we, or did we, circumvent it? We have no way of knowing when it will take place or, indeed, if it already has, an equally disturbing proposition. What do you suggest we do? You seem to have given the matter more than a little consideration."

"There is another weapon being developed by the Nazis—some sort of bomb that utilizes the very power of the microscopic atom. They are already diverting funds and their best physicists to its development. I think this is a very opportune distraction, one, we can use to steal The Bell from under the Nazis' noses and keep it in a place of "our" choosing. I can help you do it, Count. I know you want it, or you wouldn't be here. I am aware that you could extinguish me as easy as squashing a bug, but I am more use to you alive, and I intend to remain that way. I have taken certain safeguards that I will not trouble to entertain you with, but that will make it personally costly to you if you did."

The Count shrugged, "Why should I kill you?" He was genuinely perplexed. "I so very rarely have an interesting conversation with a mortal. Let us plot together."

Gerlach stared down at the chart of results. "There is something going on here that is not right, some other force outside the matrix," he muttered to himself. He started to prepare for the next test. He saw a flicker out of the corner of his eye. A man dressed in very elegant but slightly outdated clothes was standing in the corner. The man stood silently staring at the professor with the most piercing blue eyes he had ever seen. They were the last pair of eyes Gerlach would ever see.

Outside the bunker, the SS guards were not sure if they were witnessing visions from heaven or hell. Six women in the most flimsiest of garments were approaching them from out of the forest. To the soldiers, long starved of female company, it was the biggest temptation of their lives. Their orders were to shoot anything that moved outside the bunker. The SS-Unterscharführer frantically wound the field telephone to talk to his immediate superior inside the labyrinthine bunker. The SS-Untersturmführer who answered found his mouth watering at the vivid description of the women given to him by his subordinate. In this extraordinary case, he deemed that normal orders should be overruled and the women should be held as prisoners for special examination. He would take personal charge.

SS-Obergruppenführer Hans Kammler received the orders he had been waiting for from Himmler. He ordered the giant Junkers 390 ultra-long-range aircraft readied for takeoff. It was already carrying enough fuel to fly him and the device to Argentina—the destination that had been chosen at the last minute. Now it only needed his four-star presence and Die Glocke, and they would be ready for the long journey to South America. The engineer in him would be sorry to leave his precious V-2 rockets, but there was the added advantage of being temporarily, and perhaps permanently, out of the way of the war and the inevitable Allied victory and invasion. He could return when the dust had settled. The heavy-duty lifting machinery and transportation necessary for the removal of Die Glocke were ordered to proceed to the bunker.

The small room had become heady with the musky perfume of the women, mixed with the unusual amount of sweat being produced by the soldiers. The women said they had been with a traveling troupe sent to entertain soldiers at the front, and had somehow become hopelessly lost. In almost all cases, this would be a completely unbelievable and preposterous story as there were no Wehrmacht divisions for many miles in any direction and such beauties would never have been wasted on the army. But the soldiers so much wanted it to be true that they practically fell over themselves to agree with every ridiculous statement the women uttered. It was almost as if they were hypnotized ... The most outrageous lies were accompanied by the women complaining of the heat and removing more of their flimsy garments, revealing more and more of their highly desirable flesh.

All the men were suitably aroused, and their language was becoming equally salacious. The women were openly flirting now. Their leader, Angelique, was telling the lieutenant about some of the more licentious scenes in their dance routine where the women practically had to copulate on stage. Such fare was ideal for the common soldier but perhaps an officer would prefer more private settings?

She asked, unnecessarily, if his men might desire a small impromptu demonstration. The soldiers, their tongues lolling like so many dogs, watched with amazement as the women divested themselves of their remaining clothes and performed acts of simulated copulation right there in front of them, some taking the female role and others the male, and some performing both. Two of the soldiers had orgasms on the spot. The SS-Untersturmführer and the Unterscharführer were taking off their trousers—to hell with private audiences. These women needed to be interrogated physically and immediately, preferably with their penises.

The woman obliged by lying on desks, chairs, and the floor, spread-eagling their legs. The soldier's grinned and grunted with satisfaction as they penetrated the willing women, in their vaginas, gaping mouths, or anuses. Those who were not immediately guided into a ready hole were caressed gently until one of their comrades had vacated his place. It was not long before they were joining another queue—it was heaven on earth. Heil Hitler!

Then some of them noticed that the wild cries of pleasure from their friends were turning to screams of panic. What had been the most beautifully erotic dream turned into the most appalling nightmare to ever escape the sick mind of the most frenzied inhabitant of a madhouse. Wild screams of panic were followed by wails of absolute terror and submission as the women changed into their vampire form. They were adjusting and arranging their faces so they could eat—chins, cheeks, and tendons were distended to allow for enormous jaws, and lips were curled back for inch-long teeth suitable for rending and ripping raw meat apart. The jaws of the beautiful women noisily disjointed and jutted forward like those of a cobra preparing to swallow its prey. Their eyes turned bright red and glassy, like china dolls painted by a sadistic child. The slaughter was mercifully quick for the soldiers because the vampires were in a hurry. Normally, the girls would have savored the moment at leisure, reveling in each exquisite agony they inflicted, but they were working on a strict timetable.

Van Helsing strolled leisurely through the unguarded doors of the bunker as if he did not have a care in the world. The vampires had cleared the way, and evidence of their grisly methods lay all around: pieces of tattered uniforms and lumps of flesh, as if starving wild animals had just embarked on a feeding frenzy. If Van Helsing was shocked, he did not show it. He had seen enough of the atrocities of war not to be put off by the charnel spectacle. He rowed the final stretch across the underground flooded trench unhindered and reached the scientists' quarters.

The Count was waiting for him in Gerlach's laboratory. The Xerum 525 mixture was already prepared and was on the laboratory bench. It seemed to brood darkly in its glass jar like a forbidden elixir on an alchemist's shelf of deadly secrets.

The transport soldiers were confused. They had been told there would be heavy security, but there was nobody there. Obergruppenführer Kammler was naturally suspicious. He sent in an armed detachment ahead of the main corps. It was then that the earth beneath their feet began to tremble. Kammler suspected that for whatever reason, Die Glocke device was being put into effect, and he knew something of its awesome reputation for mayhem and death. The hill above the bunker seemed to disappear before their eyes as if a giant invisible hand had ripped it off. Something was rising through a furiously twisting funnel of earth and dust that had appeared above the spot that housed the bunker, or what was now left of it. The labyrinthine innards were exposed, with inmates and guards scurrying here and there like so many termites in an exposed mound. The black eye of the tornado—Die Glocke itself—as like a huge, spinning top whirling out of control. The infernal wind surrounding the defunct mine became a furious tempest. Everything surrounding the spinning Bell was caught up in the maelstrom. Soldiers were hurled around in the black tornado like toy objects, sucked into oblivion. For once, the Obergruppenführer found that the overly complicated extra-strong seat belt in the massive armor-plated Mercedes came in handy. The doors were torn off as if by a malevolent child god playing with a toy car. He watched in growing horror and astonishment as what he now recognized as the dark, dust shrouded silhouette of Die Glocke rose into the sky. It was spinning at a mind-boggling speed. Then, suddenly, it disappeared. One moment, it was there, and the next—gone. Every living thing fell back to Earth much faster than it had risen, as many screaming, broken bodies could testify.

The most pressing question facing the bewildered Obergruppenführer was: what in the name of Hell was he going to tell Himmler? That he had been slightly late, but just in time to watch the secret weapon—the weapon that was meant to end the war—disappear before his eyes? In a blinding flash of inspiration that he was renowned for—he made his decision. There were only a few soldiers left, and with them, he drove to the aerodrome and flew to Argentina, where he and the lucky few saw out the rest of the war. As far as Himmler was concerned, they had left with Die Glocke.

It was cramped inside The Bell, even for just one man and a bat. The instruments gave off a green, luminescent glow that reflected off the occupants as if they were phosphorescent deep-water creatures. Van Helsing could hear the Count's thoughts thumping about inside his head. It was as if the vampire were jumping up and down next to him in an empty room with high ceilings, where the sound was hollow and echoed in and out of the spaces within his mind. He directed the secret agent on how to maneuver the strange craft.

Van Helsing, who had never piloted even an airplane, was calm and methodical, although his stomach lurched with every sudden change of direction. He moved the controls as if he were born to fly The Bell. The Count was pleased: he had chosen well. He did not really need the instruments at all: he was using the bat's superior directional powers to guide The Bell, translating them into human terms for Van Helsing. They were moving at an inconceivable speed. Van Helsing, even though The Bell was windowless, could sense it in every fiber of his being. He did not need to look at the instruments to know it. They were heading in the general direction of Argentina, but in fact, they were heading for the southernmost point of the globe—Antarctica.

CHAPTER TEN

ANTARCTICA

Oderint, dum metuant - Let them hate, so long as they fear

From "Atreus" in Seneca's *Dialogues*.

Reich Chancellor Adolf Hitler strode about the bunker's meeting room waving his arms, and spasmodically clenching his fists. He was spluttering so much in his fury that flecks of spit covered the front of his usually immaculate brown uniform.

Albert Speer sat placidly, his arms loosely folded, his legs crossed, coolly regarding the Führer of Nazi Germany raving like a madman. He had seen Hitler have these fits many times before, but they had gotten worse since he had retreated into the bunker. The end of the war and Germany's imminent defeat looked inevitable, and so did the Führer's descent into insanity. Dimly, noises from outside penetrated down to the underground bunker, booming rumbles like the onset of a distant thunderstorm—the Red Army was on the outskirts of Berlin. As Reich Minister of Armaments and War Production, the unenviable task of bringing the news of the theft of the Nazi's top secret weapon had naturally fallen to Speer (also, no one else wanted to do it). It had been the Führer's last, only hope of conceivably winning the war, or at least brokering an armistice. Dr Morell, Hitler's personal physician, was chasing the manic leader around the room, trying to inject him with one of his drug concoctions. He could have been witnessing one of those comic farces so beloved of the British, Speer mused. But the situation was serious. One wrong word could bring all of the Führer's wrath down on one's head, with fatal consequences.

The secret weapon, known as Die Glocke/The Bell (because of its unusual shape) was arguably the Nazis greatest scientific accomplishment. Its production had been kept so secret that Speer had only the sparsest of information regarding its development. This was not surprising given that he was much more aesthetically inclined toward architecture, which took up most of his time. To have the super-powerful weapon stolen from virtually under their noses was inconceivable. Luckily, Hitler seemed to lay most of the blame on Reichsführer Himmler and the SS, and not, to his profound relief, on Speer. Finally, the good doctor managed to catch up with the madly gesticulating Führer, inject him, and commence a hasty exit with several ingratiating bows. But it still took several minutes for Hitler to calm down.

Speer uncrossed his legs and observed the miraculous transformation that slowly crept over the Reich Chancellor. It was like watching a man's mind drifting off to recollect a pleasant memory. Hitler sat down in his chair at the head of the meeting table— relaxation personified. He dismissed the retreating Doctor Morell with a wave of his hand and focused his remaining attention completely on Speer. The Reich Minister of Armaments and War Production, accustomed as he was to being under intense scrutiny, always felt uncomfortable when the Führer's blues eyes, bloodshot as they were, bored into him.

"Now, Speer give me some good news. I know I can rely on you for that, at least. Unlike those other traitors. No, I won't name them. They don't even deserve that! I won't let their foul names pollute my lips."

Speer restrained himself from telling Hitler the truth: it was already too late for any secret weapon to have saved them, anyway. It was time to make the situation more palatable for the Chancellor, tell him some half-truths. It was a time when some small flattery meant survival.

"Due to your incredible foresight mein Führer, of building several models of Die Glocke, we should have another working model up and running within a week." Speer knew full well that it would be months before one was ready. No one appeared to be completely sure how the one finished Bell had managed to take off anyway, because according to the scientists working on the project, it hadn't even been readied for launch.

Hitler clapped his hands in boyish drug-induced glee and incongruously fist-pummeled the air in triumph. "Ja! Ja! I knew it! All is not lost. Soon, we will rain terror on the Allied swine," he said, smiling beneficently at Speer as though he were a priest dispensing the Eucharist.

Speer wanted to leave there and then, but the demented Führer had not finished. "What I don't understand is who managed to pilot the Bell? Goering denies any knowledge of the Luftwaffe having sent any pilots, and the Luftwaffe have the only men who can fly such a machine. How is it possible, Speer?"

Speer, who had only heard some of the vague rumors that were circulating, decided it was best to shift the blame once more. "I am afraid you would have to ask Reichsführer Himmler about security, mein Führer. The project, after all, was overseen by the SS. There are strange rumors ... "

His voice trailed off. He knew that there was much more than just strange rumors. There had been occult practices in Wewelsburg, Himmler's SS stronghold, and the suspected involvement of vampires, of all things! Speer had his own sources when it came to Reichsführer Himmler's activities

"I know about the rumors," Hitler, said calmly. "I authorized Himmler and poor Heydrich to use whatever powers were available to them, including the occult, however evil those powers might be."

Speer restrained a shudder. He had also heard about the evil that was taking place in camps in the east, some sort of "Final Solution" designed by the late Heydrich and instigated by Himmler's notorious SS group known as the Einsatzgruppe—a euphemism for death squads.

Speer couldn't help himself, and he blurted out, "But vampires, mein Führer. Surely, they belong only in fairy tales and horror stories?"

"Speer, this is top secret," Hitler whispered, a somewhat outré mode of speech for the Führer. "The SS have been using supernatural forces against the Allies. So far, they have had limited success." Hitler suddenly had a fit of coughing. "Himmler has told me he has conscripted vampires into the Wehrmacht." He waved his hands about again. "I know, I find the whole thing unbelievable as well. Himmler is not to be trusted— perhaps he has gone mad." (Speer thought that perhaps only a madman could recognize another madman). "I want you to find out what happened to my secret weapon." He slammed his fist onto the meeting table. "And I want it back."

Speer shrugged his greatcoat on resignedly as he left the bunker. Germany was in chaos, and he was being sent on a hopeless mission. It was typical of these end days: a lunatic sending him to spy on another lunatic.

Van Helsing struggled with the controls of Die Glocke. One moment, it seemed to be in a stable position the next, it was rocking as if it were going to turn upside down. It did not help that the Count, still in his bat form, was conveying his messages telepathically. It was a method of communication that Van Helsing had never experienced before. The steering wheel was not actually a wheel but an old-fashioned yoke that controlled both altitude and steering. Van Helsing held the stick in both hands, but it was like trying to hold a fish. It slipped out of his hands with every jolt, and the Count would shriek in his mind to regain control.

It was pitch black inside the cramped hull of The Bell. The darkness was only broken occasionally by the flash of red lights that would illuminate one of the many control panels. Van Helsing tried to communicate with the Count—he wanted to know how to turn the displays on permanently. He must have gotten through somehow, although he had no idea how, because dozens of dimly lit instrument panels suddenly appeared. The weak green, amber, and red lights were just sufficient to make out the cramped interior of The Bell. Van Helsing could see the Count bat/Count sitting with its wings folded on one of the panels. Its crimson eyes seemed to be studying the flashing figures displayed on it with concentrated interest. Van Helsing was sure he had heard that bats might be blind (apparently not in this case) and steered themselves through the darkness using something akin to radar. Perhaps the Count was using a mixture of both to navigate Die Glocke. Occasionally, the Count would stretch out a clawed digit and turn a switch on or off, or press a button.

Van Helsing had been aware that the flying vessel had no porthole or window before he boarded. He suddenly felt an overwhelming desire to see outside. For the first time in his life he was feeling undeniably claustrophobic. He did, however, manage to make out the fluorescent dial of his wristwatch and happily noted that the time matched a twenty-four-hour time dial on one of the panels. Somehow, he felt this small coincidence reassuring. He also noted that several hours had passed, but what he really wanted to know was their speed and destination. Van Helsing should have known that the Count could quite easily read his mind, although he perceived it was strictly a one-way process, so the Count's answer came to him straight away. Their speed was an astonishing 1400 kilometers an hour! Their destination was no less astonishing: Antarctica! The Count anticipated Van

Helsing's next question: they would arrive in just under eight hours.

Speer surveyed the destruction. It was even worse than the reports had suggested. The launch of Die Glocke had not only destroyed most of the underground bunkers, but it had also taken half of the hillside with it. Such power! It sent a shiver down his spine. Where would this search for the ultimate weapon lead? In some terrible destruction that up to now had only been the province of God? Many of the slave laborers—mostly Jewish—had died in the explosion. But Speer had an idea of the awful conditions they would have worked under—death would have been a welcome release. The Jews would have been exterminated either way. To his shame, he was aware of that.

Not for once, he thought of the terrible atrocities that even now were being committed against the Semitic race. How would he explain himself to the Allies when they won the war which they most surely would? He would, no doubt, be tried for crimes against humanity, but he had to put such negative thoughts and the shame they would bring to one side, concentrate on the here and now. Some of the unfortunate Jews were being systematically shot by the SS, who seemed to believe that this larceny was some sort of conspiracy on the workers' part.

What was it in the Nazi pathology that so ardently believed in Zionist conspiracies?

He put a stop to it immediately, reminding the bunker commander that they would need all the men they could get if they were to repair the damage. He wondered, even as he gave his orders to spare them, how these emaciated bodies managed to cling to life. On the other hand, many of the well-fed SS guard had survived, but even these brutes seemed in a state of suspended shock.

Speer decided he needed to interrogate the surviving scientists. They were reluctant to talk at first: after all, they had been sworn to secrecy. But Speer carried direct orders from the Führer, and to reinforce his authority over them he threatened to hand all of them into the gentle hands of the Gestapo if they did not tell him what he wanted to know.

"How did whoever stole it manage to pilot the machine?" Speer asked over and over again.

Finally one of the scientists gave way. "It would not be too much of a problem to actually fly as it is pre-programmed to go to Neuschwabenland. You would just need to keep it steady, but you would also need a knowledge of advanced, anomalous physics and electromagnetic momentum as outlined by Tesla. Only someone with an intimate knowledge of its workings and Tesla's theories could start it up, and all those people are present in this room."

"What the hell has Tesla got to do with this, and where the hell is Neuschwabenland, for that matter?"

His suspicions had been aroused upon hearing the name of Nikola Tesla. He knew there were hidden esoteric orders within the SS, including the Vril and the Black Sun Society—coincidentally, the eponymous Schwarze Sonne initials were actually "SS"—who claimed that they had secret papers penned by the great scientist that had never seen the light of day. Speer disliked intrigues, especially when he was not involved in them. Once again Himmler had made him feel like an outsider. Yet why had the Führer entrusted him with this task when it was clearly Himmler's province? Hitler knew Himmler and Speer hated each other. The Führer was playing his closest confidants against each other again, a favorite game of his and a sure way to stop them from banding together and assassinating him—clever.

"Die Glocke is wholly based around Tesla's theories of endothermic explosion and Neuschwabenland is in Antarctica," the scientist said.

It occurred to Speer that he needed to get to Antarctica straight away.

"How long will it take for the Bell to reach Neuschwabenland?"

"We estimate between fourteen and twenty hours," the scientist replied.

"What!" Speer was aghast. It must be thousands of miles. He had never heard of a craft traveling so fast. He realized, with some regret, that he should have been paying more attention to what Himmler was up to in these huge underground bunkers. "Why Neuschwabenland?" he demanded.

The scientist shrugged. "As far as I know, that was the Führer's wish." The scientist dearly hoped this would satisfy the curiosity of the annoying officer. He and the others were preparing to surrender themselves to the Allies, and all they wanted was to escape from this horrible place as soon as possible. He breathed a sigh of relief when the man with the annoying questions dismissed him. He was glad that he had not had to reveal the secrets of the Hollow Earth that lay underneath Neuschwabenland.

Van Helsing was beginning to get the hang of this telepathy thing. "Why Antarctica?" He let the question form in his mind but did not voice it. He was not prepared for the lecture that followed. It was the longest that the Count had ever "talked" to him.

"You really want to know?"

The question echoed through Van Helsing's mind like he was thinking it himself. Van Helsing assured him he did.

"You won't believe it," the thought came back.

Van Helsing assured the Count he would. After all, whatever the Count told him could not be more bizarre than his present situation, he reasoned. He stopped the thought as soon as he realized the Count was laughing inside his head—he had read his mind.

"First, tell me how you came to know how to maneuver this thing."

The Count told him that it had come to him through psychometry as soon as he had come into contact with it, as he had guessed it would. When it was nearing completion he could feel its pull with each fresh experiment. It was like a feeling of ancient déjà vu even though Die Glocke had only just been invented.

He then started another strange lecture. Half a billion years ago, the Elder Race (to which the Count was merely a lately adopted son) began to colonize the Earth's solar system because their own system— Aldebaran—had become uninhabitable. These Elders or Elohin were all blonde, tall and blue eyed. The corrupt Nazi party had mistakenly adopted these Aryan traits as human perfection, not realizing they were, in fact, alien in origin.

Van Helsing couldn't help wondering how old the Count actually was. The answer came into his head instantaneously.

"I have forgotten. I have seen all the greatest of men's empires rise and fall. I have lost count of the mortal and immortal companions I have had who are long turned to dust."

Van Helsing sensed a feeling of sadness that was tinged by an ancient melancholy. The Count continued with his narrative as if nothing had happened. Van Helsing realized with awe that the Count could probably carry out many telepathic conversations and actions at once. It was taking multi-tasking to another level.

"The Elohin who inhabited Earth were known as Sumerians, and they farmed a sub-species for their food—blood. The sub-species was known as man. Sometimes, they selected one of the humans to receive their blood. These became vampires (a poor copy of the Elohin), and they eventually became Nosferatu and had powers closer to their "parents". These Nosferatu became supervisors of the farmed humans. But the Elohin got caught up in an interstellar war and called on their Sumerian cousins to join the conflict. The Sumerians left in their inter-dimensional and time-warping flying machines of which this—Die Glocke—is but a poor example. The poor deluded scientists who believe they have built The Bell out of their own intelligence have been encouraged in their delusion by the Vril Society who implanted the design in their minds using mediums who had picked up ancient Sumerian messages that had been lost in the Aether.

"The Sumerians left the Nosferatu to control the Earth vowing to return when the conflict was over. They have been gone for millennia. But millennia is but a blink of an eye to the Elohin.

"The humans bred uncontrollably. There were not enough Nosferatu to control them, and gradually, man overran Earth and chaos ensued. The remaining Nosferatu went into hiding. They managed to 'turn' some humans but most were too weak to take pure Nosferatu blood and perished, but some survived. We survive in smaller and smaller numbers. Unless we are renewed with Sumerian blood we may disappear altogether. There are very few amongst the Nazis who know about the Sumerians. Most of them are in the very top ranks of the SS. Their members belong to the Order of the Black Sun." With that, the Count finished his tale.

The whole thing sounded preposterous to Van Helsing, but on the other hand, he reasoned, he was traveling across the face of the Earth at an astonishing speed in a vehicle powered by God knows what and accompanied by an ancient vampire in the form of a bat—so anything seemed possible.

Van Helsing had a bad suspicion.

"Where were the Sumerians based?"

The answer once again echoed through his head, unbidden, as if he had thought it. But it was the Count, of course.

"Neuschwabenland, in Antarctica. It is the entrance to the Hollow Earth, where the Sumerians lived."

"So, remind me again. Why are we going to Neuschwabenland?"

"I never told you," was the Count's curt reply.

The bat fluttered above Van Helsing's head and hung upside-down on the ceiling. Their telepathic communication appeared to have ended.

Angelique and the rest of the Count's girls were getting restless—they were hungry. The Count had yet to contact her telepathically as arranged. She was the only one who the Count entrusted with his orders. Her innate sexuality also helped to keep the other girls all together. If there was one thing they craved nearly as much as feeding, it was sex. Their ensemble orgies served to satisfy their burning physical needs, and rekindle their love for each other. Angelique decided she needed to satisfy not one, but both of their needs as soon as possible. The Count had warned her about taking any of the SS guards or the Jewish workers. He had not said anything about the fat scientists though. She wandered through the ruins of the bunker, getting a lot of lustful looks from the soldiers and shy glances from the slave workers, until she came to the scientists' quarters which were relatively unscathed and luxurious compared to the rest of the bunker's quarters.

Gerlach was the first to respond to the loud knocking on the door. It was no doubt another of those cretinous SS guards, and he was fed up with their interruptions. He flung open the door only to be confronted with the most attractive woman he had ever set eyes on—no matter that she was dressed in an SS major's uniform that carried the dreaded insignia of the Black Sun. The uniform only served to emphasize the voluptuous figure that lay beneath.

Angelique did a straight arm salute and practically shouted, "Heil Hitler!" She accompanied it with an equally smart clicking of her boots' heels.

Gerlach was taken aback by this apparition and so were the other scientists in the room. Angelique strode into the room followed by the rest of the girls. The sight of the well-fed, if a trifle elderly, scientists, had set Angelique's and the other vampires' mouths watering. Once Gerlach had gotten his jaw back in place, he tried a clumsy salute and stammered a greeting. Selene, the serene half-caste vampiress, shut and locked the door behind them. The scientists were still too surprised to notice.

Angelique gave Gerlach a stunning smile and proceeded to strip. So did the others. They were down to their underwear when Gerlach noticed there was something wrong with their smiles. His greedy eyes had been occupied elsewhere. He finally hit on it. It was their teeth—they appeared to be growing. It was the last discovery he would ever make. The hunger made the vampires transformation nearly instantaneous. Gerlach let out a huge rumbling, thunderous fart—it was to be his epitaph. The scientists only had a brief moment to see all their worst nightmares come true. The beautiful women suddenly turned into monsters with deformed jaws nearly four times as large as those of a human being, jaws more suited to jackals, and their terrible maws were full of razor-like teeth. The two eye teeth were the largest, and they curled inward like ivory sabers. In fact, if the scientists had found themselves in a roomful of saber tooth tigers the outcome would not have been that much different.

The room became a bloodbath as the vampires ripped their prey apart. Unlike their cousins-in-teeth, the female haemovores did not consume the flesh, contenting themselves with licking and sucking up every last drop of their victims' precious red fluid. With superhuman speed, the girls had completely ingested all of the blood that had been in veins, arteries, on the floor, and on the walls. What was left of the scientists were mere shrunken, desiccated husks. They piled the paper-white corpses in one corner. The scientists' blood-depleted cadavers were little more than creamy white mush, as if an industrial-sized dollop of Bavarian strudel had been dumped on the floor. A pair of wire-framed spectacles sat atop the mound and seemed to stare emptily yet accusatorily at the wearer's recent unwelcome guests.

As usual, the slaughter had aroused the girls and as their bodies returned to normal, so did their considerable sexual desires— one hunger was now replaced by another. Selene and April had begun soft petting, and their deep-water musk scented the room. The others undressed in seconds, and soon there was nothing to distinguish them in the writhing mass of limbed flesh. Sounds of satisfied sighs and hissing expectation filled the room. The mass of beautiful bodies settled into a rhythmical juddering as orgasm after orgasm flowcd through them. Lust and pleasure verging on pain wracked their bodies.

Angelique, however, even through the mist of bliss, was aware that they could not linger in their ecstasy. Once all their needs had been satiated, especially those of Miss Lovelace, who took the longest, they quickly dressed and left the scientists' quarters.

It was not until they were back out in the open that Angelique received the Count's message, faint as it was. He wanted them to commandeer an aircraft and make their way immediately to Antarctica. If they couldn't commandeer one they were to take it by force. Angelique considered either option perfectly viable. They shot some soldiers who were working on a lorry. It seemed a pity to leave warm blood, but needs must, Angelique thought. They drove it to the airstrip.

Reich Minister Speer did not enjoy his flight. He always got travel sick, but it was exacerbated by being the target of anti-aircraft shells that burst in the Berlin sky like bright fireworks. Luckily, the Allies seemed more interested in invading Germany rather than shooting down transport planes, and the targeting was lackadaisical. Things calmed down once they had left Berlin behind them. Speer fell in and out of sleep. They refueled twice before they reached Argentina, where they transferred to a waiting U-Boat bound for Antarctica.

The living conditions aboard the abominably cramped U-Boat were awful. There was one toilet to service the whole crew. Its smell, along with the hanging dried meats and the men's sweat, permeated the whole U-Boat. Speer swore that once he got out of the stinking tin can he would never suffer from claustrophobia in his life. He spent as much time as he could with the tight-lipped U-Boat captain on the conning tower, gulping down the freezing air like a man dying of thirst.

Van Helsing found the flickering lights inside Die Glocke hypnotizing, and without meaning to, he started to doze off. He was rudely awakened by a shrieking braking noise inside the strange craft, and the Count's voice inside his head. The Count was calmly telling him to wake up—they had arrived at their destination.

Helsing opened the hatchway, and the Count, still in bat form, flitted out. The brilliant white light seared Van Helsing's eyes. It seemed to be coming from everywhere, and it was physically painful. He clambered out blindly and fell to his knees. Whatever he had landed in was freezing. He looked down. More light. Somewhere in his light-saturated brain, he registered that he was kneeling in snow. And he was cold—very, very cold.

The Count materialized next to him in his human form. "Are you cold?" he asked in a mildly sarcastic tone.

Van Helsing was shivering, and his teeth were chattering too much to give the sort of answer he would have liked. "How can you tell?" he managed to say, gritting his teeth. He hugged his body with both arms, and jumped up and down on the spot.

The Count, for the first time ever, touched him. He put both hands on Van Helsing's shoulders. Van Helsing felt warmth flood through him. It was like his blood was on fire. He felt full of energy. Was this what it was like to be a vampire? He put the thought aside. He had his own reasons for wishing to remain mortal and free of damnation, and it had nothing to do with religion or physical well-being.

"Let's go," the Count said.

"Where?" Van Helsing turned a full circle. There was white everywhere, white ground, white sky, and whiteness in between. They and the matte-black Bell, provided the only color in the whole frozen, virgin landscape.

"You will see," the Count set off, and Van Helsing had no choice but to follow.

Van Helsing kept his eyes firmly locked on the Count's back. The scarlet and black cloak was by far the most identifiable object on the horizon. However, it provided him with a means of conversation. He found he needed to do something with his newfound energy and talking was a way of unloading. He really felt like running, but he was afraid he might actually lose the Count if he ran too far away. Talking while briskly walking seemed the only viable option.

"I couldn't help wondering, what happens with your clothes when you turn into a bat?"

"You mean when I transmogrify?"

"If that is what it is called —yes."

"You are a mortal. You see what you need to see."

Van Helsing mulled this over for some time. It gave him something to do in the white wilderness. The Count did not seem to be inclined to further conversation.

"Here we are." The Count's voice startled Van Helsing out of his reverie.

"Here" appeared to still be in the middle of the white nowhere as far as Van Helsing was concerned. He turned around on the spot, again and again, hoping to see something, anything, but there was still nothing.

The Count did something with his hands. It was a movement that Van Helsing found on reflection that he could never recall or replicate properly. The Count's arm seemed to strobe through the air as if it was a thick, viscous material, like he was moving underwater. A low-pitched grinding sound came from under their feet. The ground began to shake violently, so much so, that Van Helsing could not keep his feet, and fell to his knees. A huge chasm opened beneath him. Its icy walls, smooth as glass, penetrated to unknown depths. Staring down into the mysterious abyss Van Helsing had a terrible sense of vertigo. It was all he could do to stop himself from vomiting. However, the Count seemed quite happy, and he pointed at something unnoticed along the chasm's walls. And then Van Helsing saw it: a staircase cut into the very ice itself, leading down, forever down.

The Count motioned him to follow, and Van Helsing followed, reluctantly at first but then with a renewed curiosity of what lay in those hidden depths. The steps, strangely, were not slippery because grooves had been conveniently cut in them in such a manner that they held their shoes firmly. The staircase of ice was barely distinguishable from its surroundings, apart from the fact that there was a slight inner green glow to it, but still, Van Helsing had to concentrate to keep his footing. He tried not to look down beyond his own feet and the back of the Count's cloak. The stairs seemed endless, and many times, he was afraid his legs would give way, but Van Helsing knew that would be fatal, and he refused with all his being to die such an unknown and ignominious death.

All things, though, come to pass—including staircases. They had reached the bottom, where there was a sort of hollowed-out pit. The Count did the same thing with his hands as he had done earlier. There was a loud crack, and then a dark line appeared in the ice in front of them. The dark line slowly spread upwards, downwards, and sideways until it had formed the outline of a doorway. The door silently slid open. There was only darkness beyond, but as Van Helsing followed the Count through the entrance, an eerie green light started to emanate from the frozen walls the same light that had illuminated the steps.

They were in a chamber with no means of egress other than the way they had come in. The chamber was drenched in cold and solemn silence. There was not even the ominous creaking and groaning from the huge crevice surrounding them. There was something special about this silence that unnerved Van Helsing, but he couldn't put his finger on it, and then he realized what was wrong—the Count was no longer in his head. Whatever, or wherever, this place was, it blocked telepathic communication. The silence between them hung in the heavy, charged air like static electricity. With alarming prescience, Van Helsing realized he missed the Count's otherworldly presence in his mind. The heat in his veins had disappeared along with the Count's reassuring telepathic voice. Did it mean that the Count was losing his powers in this unhallowed place? Van Helsing also realized that even though he no longer possessed internal heat he was not cold. The icy walls, for some bizarre, impossible reason seemed to emanate a kind of low heat.

The Count forged ahead. Then Van Helsing saw that the wall ahead of them was not really a wall—it was a green mist evaporating off the walls. The further along the passage they penetrated, the more temperate the climate became. Van Helsing felt something brushing his sleeve, and to his surprise, he found it was a leafy branch. The mist was dissipating fast, and he saw now that they were in some kind of glade. As his eyes became accustomed to the air's greenish hue he saw how picturesque his surroundings were. It was like a spring day in the Bavarian Alps but without the mountains. The air was so fresh it was like drinking from a cool, clear stream. He felt renewed and revived, but it seemed to have no noticeable effect on his companion. The Count strode along, seemingly oblivious to his surroundings. Van Helsing wanted to stop and take in the blissful, peaceful scene, but the Count seemed determined to push on.

"Why the hurry?" Van Helsing asked out loud.

"We have a meeting to attend. It would be inappropriate to arrive late after triggering the alarms. Our hosts, or more appropriately, *the Host*, is awaiting us."

Some minutes later, the glade parted to reveal a crystal clear lake banked by weeping willows and cypresses. The place could have been idyllic save for the U-boats moored incongruously along the shoreline. There was no sign of their crews.

Van Helsing saw that they were heading towards some kind of ostentatious building that looked plucked out of a fairy tale, possibly designed along the lines of mad King Ludwig the Second's Neuschwanstein Castle. He had decided quite some time ago that he was dreaming, and all of this made complete sense in a dream. It also kept him sane. The castle's drawbridge (of course it had to have one, Van Helsing reasoned) was lowered as they approached.

Inside the castle's walls, a parade of sorts was taking place of uniformed children. But this was not a parade conducted by soldiers, or if they were, they were the youngest soldiers he had ever seen, even younger than the Hitlerjugend. These perfect children would have even put the SS Division Hitlerjugend to shame. On top of that, there was not even a sign of a swastika. Van Helsing realized that over the years, he had become so accustomed to seeing it that he felt something was wrong when its very absence was conspicuous. The children were all immaculately dressed in identical khaki uniforms of shorts, shirts, and socks. They all had armbands depicting the same logo: the Deutsche Ahnenerbe. Van Helsing could see the link between the Aryan research project and the perfect children. The children, boys and girls alike, were all blonde and blue-eyed with immaculate, pale white skin—the embodiment of Aryan perfection.

"Behold, the future of mankind," the Count said to Van Helsing.

"My God, it's an army of little kids!"

"Worse, it's an army of young nosferatu raised on the pure blood of the last remaining Sumerian. Soon, just one of these 'children' will be as powerful as me. See, they are already day-walkers."

"Where are the adults?" Van Helsing asked. The sight of all the children neatly marching and then standing at attention without any spoken commands was very unnerving. "Are they all telepathic?"

"Yes, but you cannot hear them, nor thankfully, can you hear the Sumerian. Their voices would destroy your mind. That is why I have closed that channel down for you. The only need they have for adults is for food. Humans are bred like cattle and secretly replenished by Lebensborn breeding stock via the U-boats."

"Are we going to meet the Sumerian?" Van Helsing asked, anxious to be away from the unnatural children.

"Yes. I should think so. Are you afraid?"

"Yes," Van Helsing admitted immediately. "How am I supposed to feel about meeting a blood-sucking alien? your so-called 'girls' are frightening enough, and now these children ..." The fairy-tale feeling was rapidly dissipating.

The Count strode purposely forward, and Van Helsing followed. The children parted silently in front of them like diminutive white and khaki curtains. A flight of steps led up to the castle's keep. Inside, the place was completely empty except for what appeared to be an upright Egyptian sarcophagus. The sarcophagus opened by itself. Van Helsing fell instinctively to his knees. He could not help it: after all, he supposed he was in the presence of a living god or something that was as close to one.

The Sumerian was so blonde and white he looked like an albino. Van Helsing realized the Sumerian was immensely tall even from his genuflected perspective, perhaps over eight feet. The giant was naked and appeared to be sexless. But the most striking thing about the alien was its eyes. If the eyes were the windows of the soul then the Sumerian was soulless. The eyes were blacker than coal, blacker and emptier than space itself, and most strikingly they had no irises. They were like the unfeeling eyes of a china doll. The eyes were hypnotic, and Van Helsing found himself tumbling into them as if he were falling down a well that had no bottom. He was reminded of a favorite childhood book—with a young girl named Alice forever falling down a hole. If it had not been for the Count placing a hand on his shoulder, he could have stayed rooted to the spot like that forever.

The Sumerian had not moved. It could have been a statue but for the powerful force that emanated from it. The Count was also staring into those ghastly eyes, but Van Helsing sensed that some kind of unspoken communication was passing between him and the Sumerian, much deeper even than telepathy. The Count bowed very low and they left the huge, empty hall.

Van Helsing wanted to ask the Count something but the Count made a dismissive motion with his hand.

"Wait until we are out of the castle," the Count told him.

Once they were over the drawbridge, the Count said to him, "Now we can talk."

"You spoke to him, to it, didn't you? With your mind."

The Count nodded.

"Well, what did he say?"

"I will try to explain."

Speer stood in the conning tower of the U-boat, breathing in lungful after lungful of the freezing sea breeze, so cold it burned his throat. He beat his arms around his body and jogged from foot to foot. The freezing cold was preferable to the stink down below. He chatted for a while with the captain an intelligent but hard man who seemed immune to the cold around him. Their breath billowed in front of them every time they opened their mouths. The captain had informed him it was his third trip to the secret Antarctica base, but he was reluctant to elucidate on the nature of the trips. Instead, he preferred to restrict their conversation to small talk. The ice floes were becoming more numerous, and their progress became slower as they edged past huge icebergs and cliffs of ice. Thick clouds of fog surrounded the conning tower. Visibility was so poor they could hardly make out the bow of the U-boat as it nudged slowly forward.

Late that night, Speer was woken by the submerge alarm. Men were rushing to their posts automatically. They were a well-trained and disciplined crew as befitted their strict captain. Every man knew their place. Speer knew that he had to remain in his bunk. He would only get in the way. When the crew had settled somewhat, he ventured out of the tiny bunk and asked one of the crew what was happening.

"We are approaching the harbor," he was told. Speer was bemused. Surely, they should have surfaced to enter the harbor? The U-boat was going ever deeper. The hull began to creak and groan under the rising pressure. Suddenly, there was a tremendous bang. A large, flesh-piercing bolt shot passed him like a bullet, followed by a spray of water. If it had hit Speer's head, it would have taken it off. It was followed by several similar bangs. Unnecessary orders to plug the holes were screamed out. Speer breathed a sigh of relief as the submarine mercifully halted its descent and everything stopped sliding towards the bow. Evidently, they were not set on a suicide mission to the bottom of the sea.

Speer made his way forward to where the captain was poring over charts.

"Nearly there, Reich Minister," the captain said without looking up. "We will be surfacing shortly. I suggest you change into smarter clothes." Speer realized he had not shaved or changed his clothes in days. He went to attend to his toilet whilst the U-Boat prepared to dock.

Speer was totally unprepared for the sight that met his eyes when he climbed out of the exit hatch. They seemed to be docked in a peaceful, picturesque lake. It could have been a spring day on Lake Como. But the scenery was nothing compared to the welcoming party awaiting him on the jetty. There was a gentleman of indeterminate age elegantly dressed in a flamboyant white frilled shirt and black velvet cloak lined with scarlet silk, accompanied by a tall man dressed in leather lederhosen. Their companions were even more exotic—they were the most beautiful women Speer had ever seen. He immediately felt a stirring in his loins accompanied by an unwanted feeling of dread. Had he arrived in Heaven or Hell?

The elegant man stepped forward. "Hello," he said. "Welcome to the end of the world."

CHAPTER ELEVEN

THE FINAL SOLUTION

One seldom recognizes the devil when he is putting his hand on your shoulder.

Albert Speer

German architect and Reich Minister of Armaments and War Production for Nazi Germany

"Welcome to the end of the world," the Count said. He led Speer to a large makeshift hut. "You will have to excuse the accommodation. It was all we could fashion in such a short space of time. I don't think you would enjoy staying with our hosts." He pointed to a fairytale castle in the distance. Speer had to admit it looked much more welcoming than the hut. It reminded him of how much he missed Germany, Mannheim in particular, but he was never one to jump to quick conclusions. And there was something strangely compelling about the elegant man, whom he now gathered to be the Count—the leader of the vampires Hitler sought. He was also pretty sure the Count had Die Glocke in his possession hidden somewhere in this strange land.

"If I'm not mistaken it appears to be a replica of Neuschwanstein Castle," Speer said.

"Yes," the Count agreed. "But I'm afraid you would find the interior far less presupposing."

The hut was even more sparse inside. It was very dimly lit by candles. The only furniture seemed to consist of rows of coffins, a few rudimentary chairs and an equally rustic table.

"Are you preparing for a funeral?" Speer asked innocently.

The Count seemed to find this amusing. "Not exactly."

He said nothing more on the subject but led Speer to the back of the hut to another door. "I believe this is what you are looking for."

He opened the door, and there, in front of Speer's eyes, was Die Glocke!

He stared at the huge, menacing machine for an instant in wide-eyed amazement. The Count closed the door with no further comment. Van Helsing and the girls were the only witnesses present who had beheld the awesome power of The Bell, but none amongst them had been privy to how the Count had managed to get it into the Hollow Earth sanctuary of Neuschwabenland undetected. One day, it had just appeared, and they knew better than to question the Count's actions.

"If you will permit me," he said, placing a hand gently on Speer's head.

For a moment, Speer, who prided himself on his self-control thought he might faint from the overwhelming flood of information that penetrated his brain. His mind spun under some kind of spell. He suddenly knew all: Hitler's plans for world domination, Dr. Josef Mengele's malevolent influence on creating a perfect Aryan race and his subsequent eugenic experiments, the real identity of the Count, his powers, and his cadre of female vampires he called his girls. The terrible Sumerian, who lurked within the castle's walls, and his legion of young Aryan Nosferatu. Worst of all, deep inside himself, he knew it all to be true. He had heard rumors of the horrors of the extermination camps operating in the east, but like many of the other members in the higher echelons of the German war machine, he had chosen to ignore them as either too far-fetched or as exaggerated, isolated incidents. He also knew how much guilt rested on his shoulders for the use of Jewish slaves most of whom were worked to death. He found himself trembling with horror, and then he vomited profusely onto the floor. The Count looked on dispassionately at the pool of vomit and the shaking man.

"We only kill when we are forced by hunger to do so," he said. "Doesn't it make you feel ashamed to be a so-called human-being?"

Speer could only manage to nod. He had fallen to his knees and was helped to his feet by Van Helsing. He clutched to him, sensing that there was an actual man in what now seemed to him an alien and terrible world. He knew now for a certainty, if he hadn't realized before, that Himmler and Hitler were completely and utterly insane.

"What can we do?" he choked out. "It will be the end of the Fatherland. I will return to Germany and kill the Führer for the good of the German race."

"Don't worry, the Allies will take care of that if he himself does not," the Count replied. "The most pressing problem facing you and your pathetic human race is the Sumerian, who resides in the castle."

"You mean to defeat it? asked Speer incredulously. "How? It is even more alien than you, and from what I gathered from what you put in my mind, much more powerful."

"It cannot be defeated," the Count said, "but it can be distracted." With that, he invited the men to sit while he laid out his plans.

The guards at Neuschwabenland were from the Penal Regiment—the 'Sonderabteilung' (the Regiment of Death). They were unmistakable because of the black ribbon they wore on their left sleeves (two death's heads). At one time or another, they had all faced court-martials for varying reasons, the usual outcome of which was execution. If they were really 'lucky,' though, they were sent to fight in the disciplinary corps, or as it was more commonly known: the Penal Regiment.

Many died in training even before they reached them, and then it was just a prolonging of their inevitable death. They were considered an undisciplined mob by both the Wehrmacht and the SS, just riff-raff, the dregs of the armed forces, but they were also amongst the best in the world, a band of brothers in death who struck fear into anyone they came across, enemies and allies alike.

Most of the Penal Division that had been sent to guard the Jews and the other POWs in Neuschwabenland could not believe their luck. They had been taken out of the hellhole that was the Eastern Front and sent to a seeming paradise on Earth or, possibly, as they suspected, beneath it. The prisoners they were meant to guard, a mixture of Jews, Russians and gypsies, felt the same way. No one really wanted to escape, so there was not much guarding to do. As the members of the Penal Regiment were all ex-convicts themselves, they felt some sympathy for the prisoners. There was an unwritten agreement between the two parties. Both parties let each other get on pretty much with what they wanted. In the case of the prisoners, this just involved farming the fertile land, eating, and sleeping, often with any willing female (and there were plenty of those). It was much the same for the guards except they did not do any farming. The only things they missed were alcohol, cigarettes, and meat, which were unavailable. Some of them had decided to make a homemade still, but it had mysteriously exploded, killing two of them. They did not attempt to make another one.

The only visitors they ever received were U-boat crews bringing fresh prisoners and occasionally one of the inhabitants of the castle: strange, smartly uniformed, perfectly formed children. They would invite certain selected prisoners to the castle. The fact that the prisoners never returned was never questioned. The rumor was that it was some kind of lavish harem and the children were the offspring. The guards longed to be invited themselves.

Therefore, the incongruous appearance of the smartly turned-out Speer caused some consternation. Some of the guards and prisoners recognized him, and he was not welcome.

The head of the Penal Regiment, a grizzled Hauptmann, eyed him scornfully.

"And to what to we owe this pleasure, Reich Minister?"

Speer ignored the sarcasm. "I wonder if you would like to accompany me to the harbor?"

"And why should I do that?" the Hauptmann asked in return. In normal circumstances, he would have been court-martialed for daring to question such a high-ranking Nazi official. But these were not normal circumstances, and the Penal Regiment had a reputation for disposing of Nazi officials whenever the opportunity presented itself.

"I will explain when we get there. I have some very good schnapps and sausage," Speer said, maintaining all the politeness he could muster.

The Hauptmann was still suspicious, but his ears pricked up at the mention of booze and meat. One of the other guards immediately volunteered to go with them. So did a number of others.

"The more the merrier," Speer said.

They arrived at the hut opposite the harbor. Inside, it was dark as usual. The guards could still manage to make out the beautiful women sitting on coffins, though. They weren't usually disturbed, but this was bizarre even to them.

"What is this?" The Hauptmann asked, reaching immediately for his pistol as the other guards raised their rifles.

"Calm yourselves. You have nothing to fear here." An elegantly dressed gentleman appeared out of the shadows. His words seemed to instill an uncanny calmness in the guards, almost hypnotic, in fact. The Count waved them to the table, which was covered with bottles of schnapps and beer, delicious Bavarian sausage, and even cigarettes. The guards set to the unexpected feast with gusto.

Once they had satiated their hunger somewhat, their attention turned to the women.

"I wouldn't get any ideas," Van Helsing warned them. "They aren't what they appear."

"I think they should have a little demonstration," the Count said quietly.

Angelique stood up and walked slowly and sensually to the table. The guards licked their lips in anticipation. Were they to be treated to a striptease as well as the feast? Anything was possible in this fairyland they now inhabited. They could already feel their erections throbbing.

The transformation of the sensuous beauty was almost instantaneous. At one moment, they were hypnotized by her beauty. The next moment, they dropped to their knees in terror. And it took a lot to shock soldiers of the Penal Regiment. One moment, they were staring at a goddess: the next, it was a hideous monster straight out of their worst nightmares.

Angelique, in her vampire transmogrification, could sense the blood pounding through the soldier's veins, enhanced by the adrenalin of their fear. It was intoxicating, and it took all her self-control not to pounce on the living flesh and suck them dry of that precious liquid. It was only because of her mind link with the Count that she was able to change back to her human form. She strolled back to sit on her coffin and calmly commenced painting her nails.

The guards were so stupefied with horror that it took them a while, and several large swigs from the remaining bottles, to regain their composure.

"That is nothing compared to what is in the castle. The young children inside there are exactly the same, if not worse. 'They' would have shown you no mercy like Angelique here. Haven't you ever wondered what happens to the prisoners who are invited into the castle? They are just their food. Soon, those same children will be unleashed onto the world. If you think the Nazis have a reign of terror, it will be nothing compared to the terror they will unleash. They will make the SS look like Boy Scouts."

All their worst suspicions came flooding back to the soldiers. They had seen for themselves the cruelty inflicted by the SS on emancipated old men, women, and children, and even upon their own comrades. And they hated the SS and the Nazi regime they represented with a vengeance.

"What do you want from us?" the Hauptmann managed to say through clenched teeth.

"Only you and your men's cooperation," Van Helsing said. "You have the chance to give your life meaning."

The Sonderabteilung weren't much for noble causes, but something stirred within them. "Tell us how," the Hauptmann said. So, they did.

In the following days, the Penal Regiment soldiers and the crews from the U-boats formed an uneasy alliance. They both had something in common though—both groups had no intention of returning to war-torn Europe. They wanted to stay in the hidden paradise that was Neuschwabenland, and the one thing that was stopping them was who or what was in the castle. The crews of the U-boats were not, of course, trained or used to fighting on land that much. Nevertheless, they were highly disciplined, competent, and would fight to the death for their comrades. They all shared a common hatred with the Penal Regiment soldiers: they hated the SS and all it stood for. For them, the children had now become an extension of that evil.

The guards now spent half of their time training with the crew on how to fight Nosferatu, under the supervision of Van Helsing and the Count. Then, with the aid of Speer and the Count, the crews of the U-boats managed to fashion powerful bombs from their torpedoes' warheads. When the Count was not laying out his plans for the assault on the castle, he was inside Die Glocke making adjustments to its instruments and poring over Gerlach's plans for its construction and Tesla's theories of endothermic explosion, and even his outlandish views on time travel. He never seemed to rest or tire. His girls on the other hand were not only restless but hungry—just how he wanted them.

The Sumerian had briefly studied its uninvited guests as a person might study a trail of ants. They were up to something, no doubt about that. It expected nothing less after its meeting with the Count. But it had greater concerns than busy little ants. It was considering the world as a whole, and at the moment, things were going in the direction it desired, and had manipulated from afar.

Hitler's generals had given up trying to reason with their Führer. The Russians were now so far advanced into Berlin they were practically on the bunker's doorstep. Hitler had dismissed his personal physician, Dr. Morrell, and his withdrawal from his daily cocktail of drugs, once dutifully supplied by the latter, was pitiful to see.

The Führer had a giant map of the world spread out on the table in the bunker's meeting room. He had made himself the commander-in-chief of all the German armed forces since the failed attempt on his life in Operation Valkyrie. The generals he had surrounded himself with were all yes-men, not that they had much choice. If you argued with the Führer, it would mean a quick escort to the outside of the bunker to face an even more quickly assembled firing squad.

The Führer, at that moment, was stabbing the map with his shaking, stubby fingers in and about the topography of Germany. With vague waves of his other hand, he was summoning imaginary regiments from around Europe that had long since been eliminated, that would, supposedly, repel and destroy the Allied invasion. His generals nodded in mute consent. Some of them raised their eyebrows at one another when they weren't in Hitler's line of sight, but that was as far as any dissent went. They longed to get out of the bunker as soon as possible even if it meant just returning to their decimated regiments, and most were planning surreptitiously how they could arrange to surrender to either the British or the Americans, anyone but the Russians. Only Himmler remained behind when the generals left.

Hitler came straight to the point: "What is going on with my Antarctica project?"

Himmler decided it might be better to tell Hitler part of the truth for a change. He had his own plans: his own escape and survival was his main priority.

"We've had no word from the U-boat commanders, but the Thule Society has reported that a great power is building at Neuschwabenland."

Hitler waved the information away. "I have no time for any superstitious nonsense from the Thule Society right now." He thumped his fist on the table. "I want facts. I want to know when my secret army will be ready."

Himmler bowed himself subserviently out of the room. "I will find out immediately, mein Führer."

He could already hear the blasts from the Soviet artillery as he left the bunker. It was not just time to get out of Berlin: it was time to get out of Germany altogether.

The inhabitants of Neuschwabenland could hear the noise coming from within the castle as far as the bay. It was a slow, pulsing, booming sound like a heartbeat. It struck dread in every soul.

"They are getting ready to move," the Count told his assembled group. "It is time to put phase one of the plan into action."

The captains of the U-boats and their crews looked sadly toward the submarines, their homes for many years. But they knew they had no choice. The young nosferatu could never be allowed to leave that place, and the only way they would be able to get out from under the ice was using the U-boats. Unfortunately, it was the same for the humans and the other vampires, but the U-boats had to be sunk— permanently. All of them knew that they were burning their bridges in so many different ways.

Once the crews had departed to fulfill their sabotage mission, Van Helsing voiced what everyone was thinking: "I hate to be the one mentioning the elephant in the room but if by some remote chance we succeed in the destruction of the young nosferatu and their Sumerian master, it means we will still be left at the mercy of you and your girls." He bowed slightly toward the Count.

"Have no worries," the Count said in his most reassuring voice. "I will teach them to feed without killing." He had no intention whatsoever of doing that, though.

The crews of the U-boats stood mournfully on the shore as if they were attending a funeral. They had all taken their caps off, and the officers their Kriegsmarine hats, as they watched their vessels sink silently into the lake. Their spirits lightened slightly as they turned away and surveyed the paradise that might yet be theirs.

The crews joined their temporary comrades in arms— the Sonderabteilung. As serving members of the Wehrmacht they had been taught an ingrained hatred of the Penal Regiment: after all, they were supposedly traitors of the Third Reich, murderers, thieves, and deserters, but they had unexpectedly found them to be quite opposite to their expectations. The Sonderabteilung were, of course, completely war hardened, better by far in battle than any of the of the elite Wehrmacht divisions. Above all, they were pragmatic. They had been given only one choice: to fight in the most hostile environments or being instantly executed. The fact that they had lasted this long was a testament to the harsh skills they had learned. They were always sent on the most hazardous mission in the vanguard of the Wehrmacht. They were disposable—a suicide squad. They willingly passed on all they knew to the sailors and showed them how to use their weapons in ways they had never imagined.

The Count had also spoken to the prisoners and in his usual sublime manner had conveyed to them the seriousness of their situation. They agreed to help. They armed themselves with their crude farm implements and were instructed by the Count that the only chance to kill the Nosferatu children would be to cut off their heads. At first, the idea of killing what seemed to be mere children was as abhorrent to them as it was to the soldiers, but once they had realized the true nature of the monsters they would be facing their attitude changed.

The second stage of the plan was to blow up the bridge over the moat. Vampires had a distinct, sometimes fatal, aversion to water. No bridge would mean that they would be trapped inside the castle, and so, hopefully, would be the Sumerian, who had been there since time immemorial. The Penal Regiment would cross the banks in amphibious landing craft taken from the U-boats and blow holes in the castle's wall using the improvised torpedo bombs. The U-boat crews would do the same from the rear. Once the walls were breached, the ex-prisoners, accompanied by the girls would ferry across or swim to support the soldiers and sailors on both sides of the castle. The Count would transmogrify into his bat self and direct operations from above. His main opponent would be the Sumerian, who would be impervious to mere human weapons—it would be a psychic battlefield. The Sumerian was much more mentally disciplined and stronger than the Count, and the Count knew he would not stand a chance in hell against it, but he had his own plans. The Sumerian's only weakness was time itself.

The second stage of the plan worked perfectly, and they breached the castle's walls successfully, but fighting the Nosferatu children was another matter. They did not transmogrify like the girls but appeared to be simply smartly dressed Aryan youths. They moved so fast it was practically impossible to aim for their heads—their only vulnerability. The humans found themselves killing more of their comrades than the Nosferatu. One moment, a child was before them and they would aim for the head with whatever weapon they had at hand; the next moment, it was not there, and they found themselves killing another human. It was placing them under considerable distress, which the Nosferatu were taking advantage of, even mocking them at times. The children grinned and winked at the humans at every mistake they made, and the life it cost.

The girls were another matter. They had transmogrified into their vampire selves. They could move just as fast as the children and many times, they would anticipate their moves. They would be ready and waiting to rip their heads off in one swift movement. Angelique, their leader, was particularly deadly. Vampires killing other vampires was as distasteful for them as a human succumbing to cannibalism, but through example, Angelique made the others overcome their distaste and even got them to make a quick feed on each fresh kill. It made them stronger, the red-hot nosferatu blood. Even so, they were being gradually overwhelmed by the vast numbers of Nosferatu.

The first to fall was Selene. Three of the children had grabbed hold of her and before Angelique and the others could come to her rescue they had torn her apart. The girls screamed in unison, feeling her pain. The Count momentarily veered in his flight. Distracted from his mental battle with the Sumerian, he felt the dreadful loss of one of his companions throughout the centuries. It seemed for a moment that he would plummet to the ground, but instead, he screeched in vengeance as he ripped the innocent looking face off one of the Nosferatu children.

Van Helsing and Speer (the latter not used to physical battles) were in telepathic communication with the flying Count, as were the girls. They were all already bathed in blood both from the Nosferatu and the humans. The Sumerian, still within in the keep, was at the heart of the Nosferatu tactics. The Count had tried to enter the castle's keep, but the Sumerian had constructed a powerful psychic force field to keep

the him out. It radiated hatred at such an intense level
that it was as all the Count could do to keep his bat
shape. The Count, though, was proving enough of a
distraction to the Sumerian to sometimes disorientate
its communication with the young Nosferatu, and the
humans and the girls could manage kills.

The most surprising thing in the battle was
the attitude of the prisoners, especially the Jews, who
fought with a pent-up vengeance for anything
remotely associated with the SS. Their weapons might
have been crude, but they used them to devastating
effect. Scythes and homemade machetes swung to and
fro, taking off the perfect Aryan heads of the children
whenever a chance presented itself. The suicide
squads of the Penal Regiments lived up to their name:
to a man, they fought to their deaths. The U-boat
crews sank to the ground as bravely and soundlessly
as their vessels, but not before taking Nosferatu with
them. The humans' self-sacrifice, of which the
Nosferatu had no comprehension was the turning
point.

At the end, there were no Nosferatu children
left, as impossible as it had seemed at the beginning.
Of the girls only Angelique remained. She returned to
her human self, downcast and heartbroken, to join
what remained of the humans. Slipping and sliding on
blood and guts, they left what remained of the castle.

The survivors were a bedraggled lot:
Angelique, Van Helsing, Speer and a surprising

number of ex-prisoners. They had survived against all odds. All the soldiers and sailors had perished, fighting as much for each other as for themselves. The ex-prisoners sent silent prayers of thanks and forgiveness to them. The Count had returned to his normal form and joined them. They stared back at the ruins of what had once been the castle and the killing field of so many.

Then the Sumerian emerged. It flew out of the castle's keep, incandescent with rage. It loomed in the sky above them like a dark, avenging angel. Its form was surrounded by fire. Rolling thunder and flashing lightning came in its wake. The ground beneath them trembled as if it were about to erupt. The survivors could only watch in stricken awe as it approached. They stood together, ready to die as one.

And then the Count ran. The others looked on in astonishment, not to mention disbelief at the receding figure.

"No! Please, my love," Angelique could only manage to sob. She stretched out her arms in vain toward the now vanished Count—the love of her immortal life. They were Angelique's last words as the Sumerian fell upon her. Her body disappeared in a crimson whirlwind. All that remained of the Count's first and principal consort were red specks in the breeze. The others ran as if the very devil were at their heels—which it was.

The Count carried on running. Even though he felt the pain of his lost love, it did not make him pause for a second. He made it to his goal: Die Glocke. He climbed in, but instead of setting the controls to fly, he set it to the personal adjustments he had made. Tesla, in his experiments, had unwittingly created a way to travel back in time, and it was these adjustments to the controls the Count had made that he now employed. The chemicals flowed, and Die Glocke whirled. The sky grew dark around it. Time, like a river at ebb tide, slowed and flooded backward.

The Sumerian, now distracted from its enjoyment of the slaughter, suddenly realized the trick the Count had played on it. It screamed in rage and anger, and then ultimately, in fear. Speer, the only human survivor, watched in stunned amazement as everything around him started to disappear, including himself and the Sumerian. Particles of his body flew through the air to join with all the other particles of his recent comrades-in-arms. The Sumerian's, though formed a neat pile of dust on the ground. The particles formed a spiraling funnel that swept up to a black gap in sky and space where The Bell was leading it. Back in time, to a different beginning.

The SS had reached their goal: the castle of a long forgotten Count. It was supposedly the secret hiding place of vampires and the Count who led them. The Nazis, in particular Himmler, desperately wanted them on their side. No army on Earth would be able to withstand the supernatural powers they were going to harness. It would make the Third Reich invincible. But when an exploratory convoy headed by SS-Obergruppenführer Reinhard Heydrich was sent to a castle believed to be inhabited by vampires it turned out to be nothing but a ruin.

Just as the SS-Obersturmbannführer marched away to bark orders at the men to move on, Heydrich asked him, "Haven't you noticed that there is something strange about the architecture here?"

The SS-Obersturmbannführer turned around. "No, sir. Why?"

"Most of the center walls are more or less intact. It is the surrounding walls that have crumbled away. There must be something larger than just a foundation under this place. I think there are chambers underneath the center. Maybe there were once dungeons. Let the men eat their rations, and then I want them to start digging."

They were still digging by nightfall, and they had to light fires. Wolves howled in the surrounding forest. The task seemed to be getting more fruitless by the hour. There was indeed a foundation, but it appeared to be just a normal, solid foundation.

Daylight came, and a frustrated Heydrich ordered the men to stop digging.
"Just another dead end," he muttered to himself as he led the convoy away.

Underneath the abandoned dig, in a secret chamber, the Count, at rest in his sarcophagus, surrounded by the tombs of his girls was experiencing a strange sensation: the sides of his mouth were twitching, and for the first time in many centuries, he found himself smiling

THE END

39849251R00130